WORMJOB

M.T. GRANBERRY

ERASERHEAD PRESS
P.O. BOX 10065
PORTLAND, OR 97296
WWW.ERASERHEADPRESS.COM

ISBN: 978-62105-162-6

For Amanda

"For I know that my redeemer liveth, and that he shall stand at the latter day upon the earth: and though after my skin worms destroy this body, yet in my flesh shall I see God..."
-Job 19:25-26

"My milkshake brings all the boys to the yard..."
-Kelis Jones

CHAPTER ONE

BREAST ARGUMENTATION

The worms in Shari Yanisin's left breast were having an argument. Of all the world's various fat sucking parasites, *Hospitium papilla* are perhaps the most successful. Reproducing at an astonishing rate to create colonies that often number in the millions, they spend most of their lives gorging on an ever replenishing supply of human adipose tissue, expanding the resultant cavities with their ever increasing numbers. But although they are capable of speech and language, and possess a simple but effective social order built around a deeply held religious faith, the common boobworms have never been known for their great debating skills. Who has time for controversy when there are eggs to be laid, and so much delicious fat to suck?

But on this particular day a little larva had been born with a debilitating deformity. Instead of the usual oral arrangement of grasping hooks and siphoning scolex, his mouth was a ragged gash that nearly split his head in two, and was completely unsuitable for latching on or sucking. All he could do was rub his flapping lips wetly against the adiposity all around him, puling hungrily.

"Why does it look like that?" the young ones asked their parents. "Why can't it suck the fat like we do?"

"There's something wrong with it. It's not healthy and normal like we are. Shut up and suck your fat."

There were many worms in the community who felt that the best thing to do would be to kill the pitiful creature promptly, as it would likely die of starvation anyway. The trouble was, no two worms could agree on how the deed should be done.

"We could drown it!" said one.

"We could burn it on a small fire!" said another, who was ridiculed relentlessly for some time afterwards by his closest friends.

"We could crush it with a rock!"

"Where are we going to get a rock from?"

"I don't feel comfortable with the idea of crushing the baby. Let's douse it with acid!"

"Well, whatever we decide, we should do it together as a group. Why don't we just pile up on top of it and smother it to death?"

The litany of infanticide went on for quite some time, but no one could come up with a pleasant way to kill a baby, so the idea was eventually dropped. The little worm had been listening however, and his hearts were pierced by the cruelty of their words. He wriggled to his mother, tears pouring from his lidless black eyes. She pulled away from her sucking to comfort him.

"Mommies don't let bad things happen to their babies. I would never let them lay a segment on you. They only say those things because they don't realize how special you are. Your egg was the only one I ever laid that hatched. The only one! You are a miracle! That's why I named you Mikko, after the Great Worm Himself. The Great Worm is bigger than the whole world. He made everything, so we thank Him for all the good things that we have. I thank Him for you, so I gave you His name."

Mikko gazed at her in awe, and he knew then that she would never let him die. He would have given her the biggest hug imaginable if he only could. From then on he stayed by her side as she fed, and she would periodically cease gorging to regurgitate lovingly into his gaping mouth. She was his whole world.

CHAPTER TWO

A GIRL AND HER BOOBS

S hari Yanisin couldn't have been prouder of her worm-filled tits, but she gave little regard to the colony of parasites she harbored. Sometimes she noticed faint squealing and hissing noises, and little popping sounds like crispy rice cereal in milk. She had no idea what they might be saying to one another in there, since she'd never studied helmintholinguistics, and had no intention of ever doing so. The less she knew about what went on inside of her own body, the better. As long as her breasts were large and round and firm, she could deal with a little worm-chatter every now and then.

She had fretted impatiently during her teenage years, waiting for her chest to resemble those of the women in her daddy's magazines. Like most women whose tits are more interesting than they are, Shari's father was a breast-man.

"That there is what a real woman looks like," George Yanisin would gurgle as he nuzzled his bulbous nose against the glossy air-brushed nipples that stared blindly in rows around the walls of his closet. "You must have been at the end of the line when God handed out the titties!" His laughter chewed on her bones like beavers. He never failed to bring the subject up when friends or relatives came to visit. Once he even asked the pastor of their church to urge the congregation to pray for his poor impaired daughter, so that maybe God would realize his oversight and make amends. The pastor had politely pointed out that God does not make mistakes, and that maybe George should accept Shari the way she was. They never went to that church again.

Shari's mother was a voluptuous woman. Why were her puny nubs so stubbornly refusing to expand? Her father constantly offered to buy her implants, but she had an unshakable fear that if she was ever put to sleep for surgery, she would never wake up again. Just thinking about scalpels slicing her skin open gave her nightmares. She felt trapped, until one day not long after her nineteenth birthday.

She had just returned from shopping at the Grand Mall of Christ, where she had picked up a bagful of Über Bras at Jezebel's Mystique. Über Bra was the only brand she ever wore, because of their patented Better'n Nothin' jiggle-gel inserts. She turned on her TV so that she could watch commercials while she removed the tags from her purchases. Shari loved commercials. She got impatient during the regular shows. They were dumb. The people in them always had some kind of problem they had to deal with. But the commercials were good. They made her feel like the world was filled with things that would make her life better. They advocated happiness. She liked that.

"Are you tired of being flat-chested?"

Those words coming from her television struck her speechless, even though she wasn't actually trying to speak at that moment. It was as if someone had sneaked into her mind and asked "hey Shari's mind, what thing are you the most tired of?" and her mind had jumped at the chance and answered "being flat-chested!" and then they had made a commercial about it just for her. There was a woman on TV who looked just like she did! The woman was living in squalor and despair.

A man's voice was speaking with authority: "Do you long to be busty and beautiful? Women with underdeveloped breasts are widely regarded as inferior, but toxic silicone breast implants can be dangerous, and require surgery which can leave ugly scars! That's why women everywhere are turning to AUGMENTA, the patented breast enhancement process. Developed by top cosmetic biologists, AUGMENTA enlarges your breasts the natural way. Get that job, score that big promotion, earn the respect of your friends, and catch the eye of the man of your dreams! AUGMENTA makes it all possible! Side effects may include: pain, drowsiness, fatigue, weakness, dizziness, nausea and vomiting, dry mouth, slurred speech, headache, lack of muscular coordination, loss of feeling in the extremities, misplaced feelings of affection, short-term memory loss, impaired judgment, loss of perspective, antisocial behavior, short-term memory loss, depression, paranoia, drooling, hair loss, weight loss, weight gain, diarrhea, constipation, blurred vision, spontaneous cellular mutation, feelings of impending doom, bruising, tissue death, loss or increase of sensation, asymmetry, capsular contracture, pronounced nipple flatulence, involuntary eye movement, swelling in arms and legs, fever, cramping, itching, runny nose, tremor, chronic pain, long-term disability due to irreversible spinal cord injury, acid reflux, trouble swallowing, random internal hemorrhaging, urinary retention, urinary expulsion, high blood pressure, dermal rupture, feelings of hopelessness and despair, permanent brain loss, insomnia, nightmares, thoughts of suicide, delusions of persecution, confusion, paranoia, madness, and death. If you are pregnant or are thinking about getting pregnant, consult a physician before using AUGMENTA."

Shari showed her television how she could make a wonder-face. The woman in the commercial now had incredibly large breasts, bouncing tantalizingly in luxurious slow motion as she closed an important business deal. Shari saw her future in those mighty orbs. They seemed to resonate with an ancient power, unconquerable by mortal man. She knew that her father would pay whatever it cost for her to have breasts like that. She had always wanted to be that woman. Now she could be.

CHAPTER THREE

A MAN NAMED JOBS

The man sitting in front of Shari was the CEO of a major corporation. He was at once serene, intimidating, and staggeringly well groomed. He positively oozed wealth and influence. Shari recognized that he was a very important person, and she knew precisely how to approach him. She was good at her job.

"Take it all off!" the VIP requested. Straight to business as always.

Shari worked at a strip club called Big Tops, where her now gargantuan breasts were a top draw. She loved the attention. She loved being stared at. Tired truck drivers and successful businessmen alike would shuffle in religiously, putting their money down for a chance to ogle the infamous Shari Yanisin. They worshiped her, and all it took was a few thousand dollars and two injections of viable worm larvae.

Every time she heaved herself onto the stage, staggering and drooling from the pills she took to keep her parasite population in check, a man named Joe Jobs the third would be there to watch. More than anything else, Joe loved big titties. "I love big titties!" he was often heard saying, so it goes without saying that Shari had caught his eye.

"I can't believe those titties!" he confided one night to the bartender. "They're so big!"

The bartender was wiping pint glasses with an ivory towel. Joe thought he looked like a stunt man. He spoke with an accent, like somebody from TV. "If you ask me, she looks like she's got two midgets hanging off her neck. You do know they're full of worms, right?"

"They clean them first! They're totally sanitary!" Joe argued convincingly.

"She's got parasites!" the pragmatic purveyor of alcohol tongued through disapproving teeth. "She paid some doctor somewhere to be infected. It makes me want to throw up," he stink-faced.

"I'd throw up on those!" Joe uvulated wistfully. "I wish they had something like that for my cock! Like a cock-ringworm! It's not fair that women can get their titties as big as they want! She has got the biggest titties! Look at the size of them love-apples! I can't believe you don't think those are the most awesome thing you've ever seen in your life! You must be a butt-man! You'd better not be looking at my butt, man! I'll fucking kick your ass, man!"

The bartender tried to sound smart. "Actually, I was watching this show on the Learn Things Channel and they said a woman's boobs evolved to be like a butt on her chest so people won't do it doggy style."

Joe spat beer. "Boobs didn't evolve! They're boobs! They're God's most perfect creation! You can't improve that! You can only make them bigger!"

He resumed gawking at Shari Yanisin's worm-enhanced fat bags. It was too much. All his life he'd wanted to be with a woman like her, and here he was just sitting and staring at her reflection in the mirror behind the bar. What was he waiting for? He considered paying her for a lap dance, but why should he part ways with his hard earned cash just to look at the milk when he could be fucking the cow? *Because there's no way a girl like that would ever have anything to do with Joe the Janitor,* his brain suggested helpfully. Sometimes, Joe really hated his brain. He wished it would just go away and leave him alone. His doughnut eyes settled on a bottle of genuine Oaxacan mezcal with its pickled larval occupant suspended inside. At that moment he made up his mind. He was going to ask her out. Those tits were going to be his. "Fuck a cow!" he assured himself.

After the bar closed, and not before he had saturated his innards with a near lethal quantity of alcohol, Joe Jobs worked up the courage to introduce himself. "Your boobs are huge!" he said, extending his hand. "My name is Joe! I can't believe how naked you are! I could never do that!" His face exploded from smiling.

Shari had noticed him alone at the bar night after night, drinking himself stupid. There was an aching in his eyes, something almost paternal in the way he stared at her chest. She couldn't explain it, but she was drawn to him the moment she took his outstretched hand in her own. Her face exploded back.

CHAPTER FOUR

A ONE PILL DAY

Shari agreed to meet Joe for drinks the following night. That morning when she woke up, she was happier than she could remember ever feeling in her life. She wasn't sure why she was so happy. It's not like he was the first customer to ever ask her out, and he wasn't particularly good looking. But he was the first man she had ever met who displayed such an obvious *need* for her. He looked at her the way a really huge fat person eyes an all you can eat buffet, with a fresh stack of clean plates still hot and wet out of an industrial dish washing machine. It made her feel like she really mattered. She'd never felt so *necessary* before.

For breakfast she treated herself to a heaping plateful of Ready-to-Eat hot buttered lobster product (with calcium!) followed by half a box of nə-bē bärz. A high calorie diet was crucial to the success of the AUGMENTA breast enhancement procedure, in order to ensure an adequate food supply for the developing invertebrates. Otherwise, the little wrigglers might all die of starvation, and nobody wants tits filled with dead worms. That would be gross.

Still, their numbers had to be kept under control or her bust would grow too quickly and burst open, so every day Shari took two pink pills. A fresh supply was delivered directly to her door every month. The contents of the pills didn't harm the worms themselves, but simply prevented any eggs from being fertilized. They also contained a powerful narcotic to help with the back pain she experienced from carrying eighty pounds on her chest all day. She took pill number one along with her breakfast.

Afterwards Shari turned on the TV and collapsed all over her couch, drooling onto her massive bosom. She fumbled through a stack of fashion magazines. People in her line of work needed to keep up with all of the latest trends. School girl uniforms could only get you so far, and popular styles changed on a weekly basis. Not that she could just go to the store and buy any of them, of course. She had to special order all of her clothing, and it wasn't cheap. It was worth it though. She had to make sure her breasts were always displayed at their very best. Before long her vision began to blur, her chin dropped down onto her slobbery chest and she lapsed into a lovely midday coma.

The throbbing pain in her tautly stretched areolae woke her up, as usual. She rubbed the sand out of her eyes. An AUGMENTA advertisement was blurting out of her TV.

"...have recently revealed that *Hospitium papilla* secretes a hormone that prompts the host's body to produce more fat cells in the mammary region. It's a win/win situation for you and your little companions. Parents, be sure to take advantage of our new AUGMENTA HEAD START PROGRAM available to girls aged six and up."

She turned it off and wobbled free of the couch. It was time for her afternoon pill, but Shari hesitated. Joe really liked big tits. Maybe she should just skip this dose to give him that little something extra. What could it hurt?

CHAPTER FIVE

STOPGAP

He had asked her out, and she had said yes! Joe couldn't believe it. He still couldn't believe it. All day at work he yelled at himself in his head. Why had he waited so long to ask her? He could have been all over those wormy tits for months! That thought made him angry, so he screamed really loudly and punched the side of his own head repeatedly for several minutes until he remembered that he had a date with her after work. That made him feel a lot better, and gave him a partial erection.

"I've got a boner in my pants!" He informed his supervisor. Her name was Denise. She was over fifty years old, but had never learned how to smile.

"Joe blow! Get your ass in here!"

It was Mister Cozen. He liked to sit in his office and yell. Joe thought he was really good at yelling. Joe also thought that he looked like a potato with white hair, but he would never say that out loud. He slumped into Mister Cozen's office, looking doggy.

"Coming this summer, big change is in store for this little company. The fate of my nipples is in your hands." Zebadiah Cozen spoke in a perilously deep basso voice, rattling the coffee cup full of pens on his desk. He would have had a more satisfying life if he had pursued his dream of working as a professional voice actor, recording voice-over narrations for the previews of coming cinematic attractions that were shown in theaters before the feature presentation. He had opted for the rubber nipple manufacturing industry instead, and founded STOPGAP TEATS, provider of quality non-biodegradable silicone rubber nipples for baby bottles.

Joe stood across the desk from his employer, uncertain of what he should do with his hands. He alternated putting them in his pockets and under his armpits. He didn't know why he had been called in, and that bothered him. He felt very vulnerable and alone. His boner had abandoned him.

"Mister Jobs, I built this business from the ground up in the good old days gone by, working my fingers to the bone with my bare hands behind my back against the wall, uphill between a rock and a hard place both ways," Mister Cozen bloviated, amalgamating his clichés with gusto. "Until one day everything changed. All is fair in a day's work. Blood is thicker than bacon, and by blood I mean the almighty dollar. SUPERIOR INFANT FEEDING SYSTEMS is interested in utilizing my nipples. And why wouldn't they be? We offer what Mother Nature neglects to provide. Sterility! Nothing comes forth from the human body but filth and feculation. That's why my nipples are the very finest choice for suckling tots. The developing neonate requires substantial sustenance, and many a helpless mother has turned to us for aid in those first terrifying days of postpartum distress, because they know that STOPGAP TEATS give babies what they want. Babies always get what they want! If babies had teeth they'd rule the world! People don't respect you if you don't have teeth. Now, naturally the SUPERIOR people will want to come in here and restructure and reorganize things. That's what they do, and that's why they're SUPERIOR. They're going to be inspecting the whole place. If the Lord God Almighty is feeling sympathetic they won't ask to look in the basement. I'm going to have my hands full. I put a lot of eggs in this basket, and now I need to know that I can count on you before they hatch! So you and I are going to reach an accordination with each other. No more ribaldry. Do you understand me?"

Joe stared at him like a ring-tailed lemur endeavoring to interpret a dissertation on the long term consequences of malignant narcissism within cannibalistic societies, written in the one language that lemurs can't read.

Zebadiah snapped. "You're a walking liability! You know I don't expect too much from you. Not everybody is meant for greatness. You haven't got a scrap of brain in your empty head, but I promised your momma that I'd look out for you. God rest her soul. But the last thing I need is a sexual harassment allegation fucking up the biggest damned payday of my life! This company is up the creek because of that bullshit recall. If SUPERIOR doesn't take the bait, STOPGAP TEATS is going down. That means lost jobs, including yours truly! Now get the fuck out of my office, and I don't want to hear one more god damned word about your wiener!"

Joe realized then what Mister Cozen was talking about. He liked to give the girls at work what he referred to as "on-the-Jobs training." Mister Cozen had told him before that he had to stop. That had made him angry, and he had retaliated by drawing a crude but recognizable portrait of Mister Cozen in one of the stalls in the men's room doing something unspeakable with a stack of his own nipples. Joe didn't see what the problem was. He really liked girls a lot. He enjoyed talking to them and showing them how funny he could be. He also liked to tell them about his penis. Was it his fault if some of them were too dumb to know that he was being nice? He kept his mouth shut though. Mister Cozen scared him a little.

But he still couldn't not be happy. He had a date with the biggest boobies in the world. His teeth glistened as he perambulated merrily back to his station, where Denise thrust a jug of industrial grade Dər·tē·klēn at him and a long handled scrub brush. She didn't have many teeth. "What are you grinning about?" she gum-sputtered. "You'd better quit talking that shit you talk! Nobody gives a shit about you or that inchworm in your pants!" The look on her face wanted desperately to be a triumphant smile, but it failed miserably. Joe thought she looked like an old turtle.

CHAPTER SIX

TAIL SUCKER

Mikko was still very small for his age, barely three millimeters long. His mother continued to share her fat intake with him, but he just wasn't getting any bigger. To make matters worse, his deformity prevented him from speaking. He was withdrawn and shy, and so ashamed of the way he looked that whenever his mother took him out in public, he clung to the tip of her tail with his over-sized mouth, hoping to be mistaken for her posterior segment.

This of course fooled no one, and merely opened him to the derision of other young worms, in particular a pair named Splort and Tody, who taunted him at every opportunity.

"Hey tail sucker! How does your mommy's ass taste?"

"Does she poop in your mouth? Is that how come you haven't starved yet?"

They had cornered him while his mother was away. Mikko tried to turn inside out, to tuck his ugly face inside of himself where he couldn't be seen, where he couldn't hear...

"I hear she sucks your fat for you cause you can't. Does she really throw up in your mouth?"

"That is so gross!"

"Where is she now?" Splort's sucker sneered. "Did she pack you a puke lunch today? Tody, did you know Gape-mouth here was a puke eater? I'll bet he doesn't even know who his father was!"

"Neither do we," Tody interjected contemplatively.

"Splortus T. Mucum get back over here right now! What have I told you about talking to that thing?" Splort's mother usually intervened eventually, but not for Mikko's sake. She was terrified that whatever was wrong with him might be contagious.

By the time Mikko's mother returned, he was completely inconsolable. Great gasping sobs racked his body so hard he could barely breathe. Why were they so cruel? What had he ever done to them? He couldn't help the way he had been born. What did they want him to do, starve to death?

"I love you with all of my hearts," his mother said, "but no one else ever will. You scare them. If there's one thing that every worm knows, it's that all of us were formed in the likeness of the Great Worm, the creator of the world. We take pride in our connection to Him. It makes us feel like our lives have more purpose than just sucking fat day after day and making new little babies to grow up and do the same. But the eggs haven't been hatching. Entire generations have been lost, and there are many who fear that these may be the last days of the world. They wonder what it means when the only child to survive the pestilence upon us is..." She couldn't think of any way of saying what she meant without hurting his feelings, so she changed the subject. "Do you want something to eat?"

Of course he did. He was always so hungry. He opened his mouth wide... *gape-mouth*... She leaned over him and lowered her mouth to his, tenderly... *puke eater*...

A massive sob racked his body and Mikko inhaled sharply, sucking his mother's head into his mouth. Startled, he tried to pull away, but a vacuum had formed inside of his throat and the effort only drew her in deeper. He didn't know what to do. He couldn't breathe! He could feel himself stretching to accommodate her bulk inside of him. How was it possible? She was so much bigger than him! He felt dizzy, like he was going to pass out, yet still his mother's body continued its relentless descent. He thought he could hear her speaking to him, faintly. "It's okay honey. Everything is going to be okay." The tip of her tail protruded from his mouth... *how does your mommy's ass taste, tail sucker?* His lips came together. She was gone.

Mikko could not believe what had happened. His body was bulging and distended and much larger than before. He felt *full.* For the first time in his short life, he felt satisfied.

He also felt horribly, horribly guilty.

CHAPTER SIX

DINNER

"I love you, Joe. For the first time ever in my life I feel like someone really knows me. You can see who I really am. I'm just a scared little girl, hiding. But you see me." Shari applauded him with her puckered eyes.

"I can't believe how big your tits are!" Joe murmured softly, burrowing his face into the canyon of her shame. Their first date had gone surprisingly well. One thing lead inexorably towards another thing, and then that thing circumnavigated the usual bullshit until Little Joe advanced directly to Shari's thing and refused to take any calls for three weeks. Joe couldn't believe his good luck. He also couldn't believe that she hadn't asked him for money yet.

"I want you to meet my parents."

There it was. He had known it was too good to be true. He wedged his head tighter into her cleavage, pretending not to hear. He loved the sensation of the worms wriggling just underneath the skin, tickling his ears. Did life get any better than this? Joe Jobs didn't think so.

The following week, he pulled his head out long enough to meet George and Marci Yanisin. After the obligatory exchanging of names and shaking of hands was accomplished, George got straight to business.

"What line of work are you in, Joe?"

"Nipples!" Joe answered.

"Joe works at the rubber nipple factory, dad. He's a maintenance engineer."

"An engineer, huh? That's a good job! You must be pretty smart. What the hell do you do with rubber nipples? Is that something for perverts?"

"They're for baby bottles, dad!" Shari puffed.

"Oh." George batted an eyelash. "I like the real thing! I've got every magazine my little girl ever got naked in! You want to see them?"

"I want to see them!" Joe replied truthfully.

Shari interrupted. "We need to eat first! I'm so hungry! That's the best part about having fat-suckers in my jugs. I can eat whatever I want, whenever I want. What's for dinner, mom?"

"Pork chops!"

"Are they done yet?"

"What does it matter? You've already got worms! Jesus, help me! My daughter is a stripper whore!"

There was obviously a very deep and painful rift between the two women. Sensing this, Joe attempted to diffuse the situation. "You've got really big tits too, Missus Yanisin!"

"Well, I got mine by having babies!"

"Mom! I told you I take deworming medicine to keep my tits from exploding! It wouldn't be good for a baby!"

"You should just take the whole bottle and get rid of the mess of them," Shari's mother suggested hopefully.

Shari was bomb-shelled. "That would kill me! You want me to die?"

"I want you to stop rubbing your tits in the face of every low-life who wags a dollar under your ass and start thinking about putting those things in my grandbaby's mouth instead!"

Shari made a face with her face. "Gross! That's perverted! You shouldn't put a sex organ in a baby's mouth! People who do that ought to be arrested for baby-rape!" She hoisted her breasts onto the table and sat down.

"You're going to break my grandma's table with those things. I'm never going to have grandchildren because my daughter's an idiot!" Marci Yanisin spat and set a plate of abused looking gray pork chops on the table, next to a bowl of extruded potatoes and something brown and shiny.

Joe ate heartily. "I don't ever want to stop eating this!" he beamed. Shari didn't eat much at all.

After dinner, the four of them watched an Irving Berlin biography. Shari's mother loved Irving Berlin. "I put one of his songs on my phone for your ringtone, mom," Shari mentioned meekly. Marci Yanisin remained firmly scrunch-mouthed. Shari wanted more than anything at that moment to give her mother a hug, but she hadn't been able to do that for years.

Later that night after returning to her apartment, Shari stood naked in front of a mirror regarding her body critically. Her breasts still weren't as enormous as she wanted, though her right one looked slightly fuller than the left. She'd been skipping her medication a lot. "Only two more letters in the alphabet," she reminded herself quietly. Then she felt it.

"Joe! Joe, I have a lump in my breast!"

"I like your lumps!" he said as he wrapped his arms as far as he could around her from behind and snorted her cereal colored hair.

"This is serious, Joe! What if it's cancer?"

"You worry too much!" Joe said, taking off his good blue jeans that he only wore on special occasions. "Come get in bed! You can't just stand there playing with your tits and not expect me to get all worked up!"

"Joe, I'm really scared!"

"It will be okay! I won't ever let anything bad happen to you! You're freaking yourself out about nothing! Now come on over here and wrap those wormy boobs around *this!*"

Little Joe concurred wholeheartedly with his suggestion. One hundred and eighty seven seconds later, millions of sperm cried out in terror.

CHAPTER SEVEN

WORM AT LARGE

The lump in Shari's breast was Mikko. Since the day he had inadvertently eaten his mother, he had developed a taste for his own kind. They were soft and slippery, and went down easily. He was getting huge on his high protein diet, and with every meal he got a little bit larger, and a lot more confident.

Splort and Tody had been among the first to go. He was surprised to find that he didn't really feel very good about it afterwards, but then he had never felt good about anything in his life. At least they couldn't laugh at him anymore.

Gape-mouthed puke eating tail sucker...

He was very careful not to be observed when he ate, but he couldn't hide the fact that he was growing so rapidly. There was a rumor going around that he had overcome his deformity and had discovered an accumulation of deeply buried visceral fat. The older worms occasionally speculated about these sorts of deposits, but none of them had ever actually found one. They were annoyed that he might have achieved what they couldn't, and was keeping it to himself.

Mikko used this to his advantage. He would slip away from the main group every day and go off on his own someplace out of the way and private. Inevitably, some suspicious individual would follow him to see for themselves whether he had indeed discovered a previously unknown cornucopia of delectable fat. Mikko always swallowed them head first, so they couldn't cry out a warning to the others.

The absence of so many worms did not go unnoticed, and before long a new rumor emerged: "He's sharing with them, and they won't divvy up with the rest of us! They'll keep it all for themselves!"

Soon they came in droves.

CHAPTER EIGHT

BELLY BUMP

She had lost track of the suspicious lump, but one morning while performing her now routine weekly breast examination on herself, Shari lifted her forty pounders up over her shoulders and looked at her belly for the first time in two years. It was swollen.

"Joe, I think I may be pregnant!"

"God! First cancer, now this!" Joe responded linguistically. He was good at talking. His momma had told him so all the time, but she was dead now so she couldn't tell him anymore, but he remembered her telling him a bunch of times what a good talker he was. He finished his beer and left to go to the bar by himself, so he could drink some beers and talk things out with himself alone with whoever was at the bar.

When Joe left, Shari felt sick to her stomach. She lumbered to the bathroom and kneeled in front of the toilet, but her tits were so big she couldn't reach the bowl and she vomited into her cleavage.

In the shower afterwards, she washed the remnants of

her breakfast off of her bulging belly bump. She hadn't had a menstrual period since her procedure. Was she really going to have a baby of her very own? Her mother would be so happy! What about her worm-pills? Would she have to stop taking them completely? What if they hurt the baby? What if it came out all deformed and they had to put a bag on its head when they took it out in public? What if it expected her to feed it milk out of her body like some kind of human cow? She would never do that! Her baby was going to get nothing but the best artificial milk from clean plastic bottles. Joe could bring home plenty of rubber nipples from work. But even then, she would have to take the bag off of its head and people might see it! At that moment Shari made up her mind to stop taking her medicine right away so that her baby wouldn't be born embarrassing looking.

In the ensuing weeks Shari's worm population exploded, and her breasts would have also if Mikko had not been so ravenously hungry. It was his corpulent rope-like body coiled within the fatty layer between her abdominal muscles and skin that was causing her midriff to swell. He no longer fit comfortably within the connective tissue of her mammary glands. When he was hungry, he simply extended the front portion of his head until it was slender and tapered, and sucked worms out of her breast by the hundreds, like an aardvark raiding a termite mound. He fed exclusively from the left breast, since they were the ones who had threatened to kill him when he was only a baby. They had always been afraid of him. Now they no longer had any illusions about what he really was.

Shari began picking out names.

CHAPTER NINE

LEAVING

"This is a titty bar, not a freak show!" was just one of the many eloquent sentences employed by Shari's boss when he terminated her employment at Big Tops. Since she had stopped taking her pills, her left breast had shriveled up like a twenty pound skin-raisin, while her right one had grown to triple its previous proportions, making it extremely difficult for her to walk without the use of a handy collapsible cart she had purchased at a yard sale.

Joe was ecstatic. "I want to bounce on it like a bouncy ball!" he said in his excited voice. Shari wouldn't let him though, out of concern for the baby. Also, her feelings for him had changed in the preceding months. She still had feelings for him; they were just all bad ones. She had been thinking very seriously about leaving him.

Joe took some time off from work to help her prepare for the imminent birth of their child. Actually, Mister Cozen had politely demanded that he stay away from the plant while the inspectors from SUPERIOR INFANT FEEDING

SYSTEMS were performing their review. Joe didn't mind. He had been looking forward to painting the nursery, and now he finally had the free time. They had argued about it, but he insisted on a monkey theme. "Boys love monkeys!" he explained to her carefully.

Shari conceded to the monkeys, but was determined to have her say in naming her firstborn child. She agonized over the multitude of possible choices. Whatever she chose, the kid would be stuck with for life. It was a rather daunting prospect.

Joe didn't see what the big deal was. "We should name him after me and my dad and my grandfather!"

"Joe? What does it mean?"

"I think it means normal! Like average!"

"Average Joe?" Shari snarled her nose and executed a glob of monkey colored paint on the wall. "Don't you think one Little Joe in the family is enough? I think names should mean something important. What if it's a girl? My mom is going shopping tomorrow to buy us all the stuff for the baby, and she wanted to know what colors to get." Her right nipple made a spluttering wet flapping noise underneath her extra, extra, extra, extra, extra, extra, extra, extra, extra large t-shirt.

"Your titty farted!" Joe was overwhelmed with conflicting feelings of humor and concern. It was a challenging moment for him emotionally. He was proud of himself for only laughing a little bit. "Maybe you should go see a doctor!"

Shari turned brick. "I don't need a doctor to tell me I'm pregnant! I can feel it kicking! Women have been having babies for hundreds of years. I'm just leaking milk! Look!"

She flashed her boob at him. A glistening white line oozed from her right nipple, which was puffy and red like a raw hamburger.

Joe barf-swallowed in his mouth. "That's not milk! You've got worms coming out of you! You need to go to a hospital!"

"God, you sound just like my mother! I'm not going to a hospital! I'm not sick! My immune system is making the worms go out so it will be good for the baby! I read it in a book! I'm not going to get locked in some little examining room with some pervert in a white coat sticking his fat fingers in me! All doctors are psychos who like to cut people open to see how they work inside! Cut them open like experimental monkeys! I'm done doing this!" She stuck her brush back in the paint can, where it would ultimately dry into a rigid brown fin. Her monkeys looked better than Joe's did. His looked like mutant squirrels.

That night Joe couldn't sleep. Shari was snoring louder than a rampaging giant monster of the atomic age smashing buildings in Tokyo, and her stomach area was thrashing like a bag full of alcoholic cats. She had been so hot before. Now she never let him have any fun, and she talked all the time. But that one booby was so big! The biggest in the world probably, and it was all his! He didn't really care about the rest of her body. He lay on his back and stared up at the tremendous fleshy sphere looming over him. It seemed to be calling his name. *Joe. Joe! Ride me like a horsey! Bounce on me! What she doesn't know won't hurt you!* He'd never be able to sleep with that voice in his head, and he had a boner like a hard-boiled egg. He couldn't wait to tell the girls at work about it.

Before his sleep-starved brain had time to intervene and ruin everything, Joe clambered up and straddled Shari's boob, being careful not to step on the baby. He was up so high! The fizzy tingling of the worms inside tickled his bare ass and scrotum. It reminded him of the time after his mother had died when he was still a kid and he had gone to live with his uncle, and his uncle had made him sit naked on the air conditioning unit behind his trailer and masturbate with him. But that didn't really happen.

He began to grind his tumid organ rhythmically against her boob-skin. Her nipple glistened tantalizingly inches in front of him. He had been bottle-fed as a baby, and had never known the taste of his own mother, so now Shari's nipple challenged him with its mysterious allure. It was his master, and he was its slave. He worshiped it. He bowed his head down and rubbed his face all over it. He wanted to join with it, to wrap himself up in it like a nipple-blanket. It was the only thing that mattered in the world. It amazed him that something so small could consume his mind so completely. He fell asleep up there, like an infant safe in the comfort of a mother's bosom.

Within that giant tit there were murmurs of genocide. The left breast was now a barren wasteland, and the smattering of refugees who had managed to escape and make the dangerous journey to the right one arrived telling stories of a monstrous aberration that devoured all in its path. The stories acquired an almost religious fervor in the telling, and many worms clustered together, praying for deliverance.

For some it was simply too much, and they at once made preparations to leave. A steady food supply was not worth their lives or the lives of their children. They made for the nipple, where they could exit the body and seek a safer host. Splort Mucum's mother was among them. She had already lost one son; she couldn't bear to lose fifteen hundred more.

They exited a thousand at a time, to avoid attracting attention.

CHAPTER TEN

EAT AT JOE'S BRAIN

The human brain is about sixty percent fat. Had Joe Jobs been aware of this fact, he might have thought twice about dozing off with his nostrils pressed squarely against Shari's nipple. As he snored obliviously, an abrupt eruption of worm-milk tit-farted into his nasal cavity. Lost and disoriented, one thousand displaced parasites pushed blindly up into his cranium, penetrating his brain.

"The Great Worm has delivered us to this place! Truly, we are saved!" they cried, and began burrowing in to the invitingly soft tissue of their new home.

CHAPTER ELEVEN

TAKING STEPS

Shari woke up jumping with hair in her face. She had been dreaming. In the dream she had been naked. Her breasts were small again, and her body was normal. She was wandering alone in a dilapidated subway station. It wasn't any place she had ever been before.

She picked her way carefully down a dark and heavily littered stairway, hesitating on every step. The railway platform at the bottom looked more like an underground garbage dump.

She heard muttering in the darkness, and realized that one particularly foul looking pile of trash was actually a man. The man was dressed in a robe made of rotting bed sheets and plastic bags, camouflaging him amid the heaps of rubbish. He was wearing sunglasses, which Shari thought was odd given how dark it was, until she noticed that he didn't have any eyes. His trembling dirty gray hands clutched a cardboard sign that shouted THE END IS NIGH in crawling black letters.

The man began dancing around in large cloddish circles,

shouting in a voice like spoiled cabbage. "The end of the world is where He stands! We all get on a train! We go in a circle! We all get thrown up back where we started! The world is going to end again! The Divine Consumer will eat His tail!"

"That doesn't make any sense," Shari said in dream words. "What does that have to do with anything?"

"Nothing," he grinned upside down. "I don't remember where I am half the time. You're naked! Hey, you want to see what I got?" He thrust one grimy hand down the front of his pants and pulled out a shiny red apple. It looked delicious. "Put that in your mouth!"

Shari shook her head. There was no way she would eat anything down here, no matter how good it looked. Not even in a dream. It was probably rotten on the inside.

The man shrugged and took the best bite that he could with the few teeth that he had. He chewed slowly, obviously relishing the flavor. "That tastes good in my mouth! Ain't no worm in that! Don't you know it's rude to keep the dead waiting? Worms are the army of Death!"

Decrepit red curtains closed suddenly, concealing the blind man from her view. She pushed through the material, only to find herself outside on a crumbling asphalt parking lot in front of a large black circus tent. A man with three hands was washing a horse with no legs. Her boss from the strip club was standing on a wooden platform like a gallows, dressed in barker's garb and shouting into an octopus megaphone.

"Hurry! Hurry! Step right up! See the disgusting freaks we have assembled for you under the big top! If you have a weak heart, bad nerves, or expect a baby, step inside this exhibit at your own risk!"

"How much is it?" Shari asked him.

"Talent doesn't pay!" he wink-faced at her, and ushered her into the tent.

Shari shuffled her bare feet through a thick layer of sawdust covering the ground. There were cages everywhere. Her mother was inside one of them, sewing her vagina closed with a catgut string and singing "No more whores from the glory-box, oh Lord!" at the top of her lungs. In another cage her father was squatting on top of a concrete pedestal with a curly blonde wig on his head. He was covered from head to toe with breast-like sores, and he kept rocking forward and back while grunting "You're not a woman, you're not a woman, you're not a woman, you're not a woman," over and over again under his breath.

She looked down at her own breasts. Her nipples had inexplicably protruded like massive erect penises. Joe was there in the dream. He was also naked, and his head was twice its normal size. He pushed her onto her back and sat straddling her with his butt on her chest. She found the whole thing repulsive, but nevertheless her dick-nipples eagerly took turns erupting worm filled ejaculations into his lower intestine.

As he clambered off of her, she realized that she was in a cage now, too. She was a freak. Tired truck drivers and successful businessmen shuffled in to the tent, putting their money down for a chance to ogle the infamous Shari Yanisin. The woman from the AUGMENTA commercial strolled leisurely in, accompanied by the doctor who had performed Shari's procedure. What was his name? She couldn't remember, but she called out to him "Fix me! Please make me normal again!" He turned away from her, counting the money from the door and laughing through heckling teeth.

"A woman without breasts is not a woman at all," his teeth taunted. "Look, you've gone and gotten your boyfriend knocked up!" Shari had noticed that big-headed Joe looked like he was trying to smuggle thirty kilos of something in his colon, but she protested. "No! *I'm* having a baby!"

Something splatted on the floor at her feet. Shari glanced down between her limp dream-penises. A pale glistening tapeworm as thick as her finger was rubbing its head against her big toe, purring like a kitten. It had the squinched face of a newborn infant. She shuddered.

Spletch! Splat! Two more chubby worms fell from the

shadowy black canopy overhead. Shari stepped back. These were monsters compared to the tiny ones she had been injected with. Several more fell. They all had baby faces.

"Mommy!"

"Momma! We missed you!"

"Dance for us, momma!" they pleaded, contorting themselves like limbless gymnasts and mewling encouragingly.

"I can't dance anymore." Shari said with a sad little smile. "I messed myself up. No one wants to see me dance. I'm not a real woman anymore."

The worms were emphatic. "We'll pay you! We don't care if you dance good! Show us those titties, momma! We're hungry for a show!"

"I'm sorry, but I just don't feel like dancing right now."

The worm children lashed at her feet discontentedly. "You're not our mommy! Our real mommy would never tell us no! She would give us whatever we want! Our real mommy loves us. She would do anything! She would sacrifice herself for us!"

A shadow passed over them. Something was swinging back and forth above her head like a pendulum. Shari ducked and squinted upwards to see through the glare of the gelled lights that were shining in her eyes. A bloated tapeworm fell and splattered on her face. She spaz-handed it off with revulsion.

The big-headed dream Joe began howling as dozens of full term giant worm-babies suddenly escaped his anus. The new arrivals promptly joined the mob that was strangling Shari's ankles.

The shadow passed again. Whatever it was had dropped lower and she could just make it out. It looked like a giant moth or a butterfly. Shari didn't know what the difference was. It smelled like rotten meat. It was whimpering.

Hands grabbed her from behind. Shari flailed to get away, to see who was holding her. The rotten meat smell was getting stronger. Her mother's voice rasped hotly in her ear.

"Look what you've done to yourself! You were such a dear little girl!"

She felt her father's mammarian pustules pressing against her back. Why wouldn't they let her go? She didn't belong to them anymore. She opened her mouth to scream, but no sound came out. Her father's sores and the wriggling cherubs screamed for her.

There was an answering cry from overhead. Shari heard anguish and hopelessness in that cry like she had never heard before. The swinging creature was not a butterfly or a moth. Restrained inside something that looked like a wrought iron ribcage hanging from chains was a withered and frail old woman. Her head was fastened securely upright, held in place by screws penetrating the skull behind her ears. What Shari had at first mistaken for wings was in fact yards of extra skin hanging under her arms like bruised meat curtains obscuring most of her lower body, except for the bluish tips of her dangling feet.

"Is that supposed to be me?" Shari wanted very much to wake up.

The horrible old Shari sneered. Worms were spurt-pouring out of a festering black hole in her sternum, and her rotting torso exploded open like a piñata filled with squirming candy. There was nothing inside of her but the worms.

Shari woke up jumping with hair in her face. Joe was asleep next to her, drooling into her armpit. His nose looked puffy and red, and his eyes were moving rapidly beneath his eyelids, but his head was its normal size and there didn't seem to be anything wrong with his butt. She left him lying in his wet spot and put on the only dress she had that fit her anymore. She knew what she had to do.

She hoisted her bloated boob onto her cart and wheeled herself out of the apartment as quietly as possible. She took the elevator as always. She refused to even acknowledge that her building had stairs, since she hadn't been physically capable of using them in years. They were just one more thing she had left behind, along with that flat chested girl she used to be, clothes that fit properly, adequate personal hygiene, and hugs.

Once out in the street, Shari began the long slow wrestling match that was necessary whenever she went anywhere these days. She didn't fit in her car anymore, so she scooted bravely down the sidewalk one deliberate step at a time. Women and men alike stared in shock and horror at her, but she was oblivious to their revulsion. *They're jealous,* she thought.

"Mommy, what happened to that lady?" a tiny orange haired girl asked her mother as Shari passed by like a fleshy parade float.

"There's just something wrong with her, honey. Don't stare at her. Finish your sandwich."

Shari stopped dead in her tracks. The girl's mother was sitting on a public bench in broad daylight breastfeeding a baby boy! In front of her own daughter! Shari couldn't hold her tongue.

"That is disgusting!"

"Excuse me?" the woman replied cautiously, cuddling her infant son securely to her chest and casting a wary glance at her daughter, who was eating a peanut butter and jelly sandwich, oblivious to the avalanche she had just triggered with her innocent question.

Shari laid into the young mother. "There's nothing wrong with me! You should be ashamed of yourself! Nobody wants to see your scrawny quarter pounders hanging out! I break my back showing my tits for cash, and you're sitting here just as pretty as you please giving every Johnny- Jack-off in the street a free show! What's wrong with you?"

The woman had been through something like this before. "Where do you work, at the circus? Maybe if you got that fixed you could get a real job. I mean, what do you have to be proud of, really? You've been brainwashed by society and the media and men into believing that the size of your tits is actually something to be proud of, when you were either (a) born genetically predisposed to having big tits, in which case it just happened to you and you didn't do anything to achieve it, or (b) you paid some doctor somewhere to do this to you.

I assume whatever is under that tent you're wearing isn't natural. Is that what you think it means to be a woman? For your information, nursing a baby is the most natural thing in the world."

Shari was livid. "Oh, is it all natural? That's great. Why don't you just take a shit right there on the bench while you're at it? It's okay! It's totally natural! Natural doesn't mean normal! Tornadoes are natural! Great white sharks are natural! Don't you know that there are people in this world who make rubber nipples for a living, and they have children too? How can you be so selfish? Don't you know that every time you do that you're taking food out of my baby's mouth? My life is falling apart and you're sitting there molesting a baby! You want to nurse somebody? Go to nursing school, you selfish bitch!"

Shari turned her back on the woman and trudged proudly away, shoving her breast ahead of her like a morbidly obese and limbless giant infant sucking the life-force out of her chest, her cart squeak-wheeling under the strain.

CHAPTER TWELVE

MANFINGER

Without any warning or appointment, Shari Yanisin charged dramatically into the crowded lobby of AUGMENTA BIOLOGICALS. She could barely contain her spittle. "I have to see Doctor Manfinger right now!"

The roomful of waiting women rubbernecked spitefully, their hopes of enhancing their busts momentarily rattled by doubt at the sight of Shari's deformed body. A too perfect looking woman hurried to subdue her. "Ma'am, I'm going to have to ask you to please keep your voice down."

Shari was lizard faced. "I'm not going to keep my voice down! Doctor Manfinger has to fix this! He's the only one who can make me beautiful again! He made me a woman! He made me a woman and I need him to make me a woman again! Tell him! You tell him he has to make me a real woman again!"

The roomful of remediable females was becoming anxious. Two young ladies who had been sharing feelings of uncertainty prior to Shari's entrance agreed without audibly communicating that her appearance was a sign, and slipped quietly out through the emergency exit. Those who remained were grousing irritably to one another.

The too perfect woman muzzled Shari with spit-polished eyes. "Okay. I'll tell Doctor Manfinger you have a special emergency, but only if you sit quietly. We're very busy today, so I'll have to put you in the children's lounge. I think you'll fit in there."

Good! Finally someone was taking her seriously! For the first time in months, Shari felt like things were in her control. She wasn't going anywhere until she was seen by Doctor Albert Manfinger. He was the only doctor she had ever trusted. He had administered her worm injections himself. He would know what to do.

She took in the children's lounge in a single sweeping gawk. It was the pinkest room she had ever seen in her life. It reminded her of her favorite aisle in the toy store when she was a little girl. The one with all the dolls. She parked her cart in a corner and leaned forward onto her giant breast to take some of the strain off of her back and legs. The pressure made her stomach gurgle.

There were only two girls in the room, both accompanied by their mothers. One of the women was dabbing at her daughter's soggy face with a tissue. The tearful girl looked about seven years old.

"You're going to be so beautiful when they get done. Don't you want to be pretty like mommy?"

Her daughter didn't say anything, but was peering pitiably at the other girl in the room, who Shari thought was probably eleven or twelve years old. She had her arms pretzeled in front of her, but they didn't conceal the fresh blood stains transfusing her shirt on both sides of her chest. This girl's mother was talking on her phone. "We're down here at the AUGMENTA office. Yes, she's getting it. I wasn't going to let her have it, but then she tried to do it herself. Styrofoam balls!

She did a pretty good job, but they had to take them back out. A utility knife. I know! I told him to keep that stuff put up, but he doesn't listen to me! That's what I said!"

Shari couldn't look at them anymore. She scanned the room for something to keep her mind occupied while she waited. There weren't any magazines in this part of the waiting room, but there was a small television mounted in one corner near the ceiling. She didn't recognize the show that was on. Four preadolescent girls were hanging out together in what looked like an oversized tree house. One of the girls was Hispanic, one was Asian, one was black, and one was white. All four were huddled around a felt hand puppet that looked like an oversized caterpillar. He was cute and fuzzy, and didn't look remotely parasitic, but Shari knew immediately what kind of worm he was supposed to be. He was attempting to glue together match sticks and construction paper, but was having difficulty due to his lack of limbs, so the girls were helping him.

The worm spoke in a chirpy falsetto. "Oh, thank you! I was really having trouble."

"It's okay H.P. We're happy to help," said the black girl. "What's wrong? Why do you look so sad?"

H.P. the Worm hung his head. "I need a place to live. You guys have such a great tree house, but I can't stay here. I can only live in one special place, and it's inside of you... right next to your heart. I'd be more than happy to help out once I move in! I can help you to grow up and be pretty! I'll bring my brothers and sisters! There are enough of us for all of you! We'll all pitch in! We can do it together!"

The white girl nodded like a robot. "Of course we'll help you, H.P. We're best friends, and that's what best friends do! They help each other!"

Shari couldn't quite believe what she was watching. The constant demand of the millions of hungry worms feeding inside of her had never struck her as being particularly friendly.

A man wearing a white lab coat walked into the televised

tree house carrying an acoustic guitar.

"Who wants to be pretty? Raise your hands!"

Three of the girls raised their hands, but the Asian girl looked skeptical. "Are you sure it won't hurt?"

The doctor grinned the biggest, whitest grin Shari had ever seen in her life, and began strumming an exuberant rhythm on his guitar. "Don't worry, little lady! I'm a doctor! Doctors don't hurt people. We make people better. In fact, with just one simple procedure, we could make you better than everybody! He started to sing:

> *"Bigger, better, best!*
> *The worms go in your breasts*
> *They'll grow right on your chest*
> *Until they're bigger than the rest*
> *Bigger, better, best!*
> *Your friends will be impressed!"*

The guitar doctor was on a roll. The four girls joined in the song with well rehearsed bravado.

> *"Now if you want to be happy*
> *Then the thing you've got to do*
> *Is go and see the doctor*
> *Let him add a thing or two..."*

"Shari Yanisin? You can come back now."

Conflicted by her desire to watch more of the program, Shari begrudgingly dropped back down onto her feet and dutifully followed a pretty black woman with a clipboard. She was impressed at how attractive all of Manfinger's employees were, and wondered if they were hired solely for their looks. Behind her on the small television, the children's program started over again from the beginning. It played on a loop, over and over all day long, allowing H.P. and the medical minstrel to persistently worm their way into the hearts and minds of malleable young girls.

She was escorted to an elegant private room, where she was seated in a very comfortable chair. A nurse shoved a plush chaise longue beside her so that her grotesque boob would be comfortable too. Greco-Roman marble statues of goddesses stood in graceful poses along the walls, and a glass aquarium occupied one corner of the room. There were no fish in it.

"It's wonderful to see you again Shari," Doctor Manfinger said with no obvious enthusiasm when he entered the room thirty five minutes later. He was an imposing man, cut like a wooden Indian. Shari thought that he looked like someone from a soap opera. He spoke in a relaxed voice that seemed somehow unnaturally amplified in the small room. "I spent an hour this morning before work reading quotations. I wanted to greet each of my patients with some prepared anecdote about beauty or perfection or the meaning of womanhood, but it's been so busy here today I can't remember what I had for breakfast. So tell me, what did you need to see me about this morning?"

Shari was baffle-mouthed. "One of my boobs is bigger than I am and the other one shriveled up and died!"

The doctor regarded her lack of symmetry dispassionately. "We spoil what we have when we desire that which we have not. I'm paraphrasing. There's no need to worry. It's perfectly normal to feel ashamed of your own body, especially for women of your age. You don't have to feel guilty about being ashamed. Mankind was created in the image of the Almighty. Women, regrettably, came about as more of an afterthought. But what God neglected, we here at AUGMENTA BIOLOGICALS can nurture and sculpt and bring forth to perfection.

In my life I have aspired to great things. I achieved them by focusing on the little ones. You haven't been taking your medication. You do recall that this organization cannot be held legally culpable if you fail to follow the post procedural conditions laid out in the contract that you signed prior to your AUGMENTA procedure?"

Shari was caught off guard by his accusatory tone. "I quit taking it because I'm expecting!"

Manfinger shook his head. "You can't get pregnant, Shari."

"Oh, yeah? If I can't get pregnant, what is this in my stomach?" Shari queried.

The doctor considered his answer carefully. "Evolution," he said. "You are much more than a woman now, Shari. You have donated your body to a higher purpose."

"Stripping?" Shari laughed.

"Science!" His answer stole the laughter right out of her mouth. Shari had barely passed science class. Manfinger extorted his face. "Whether you realize it or not, you have become an incubator for a new species. Your body is now a launching pad for new life! You should be proud! Let me ask you something. There was a woman who assisted you in the waiting room. How old would you say she is?

"I don't know. Thirty?" Shari ventured.

Manfinger smiled a backstairs smile. "What if I told you that she has worked for me for over thirty years, and is due to retire next month?"

Shari was hammered. "That's impossible! She doesn't look any older than me!"

The doctor elaborated. "Breast augmentation was only the beginning. Our philosophy at AUGMENTA BIOLOGICALS is that nature can solve any problem. You just have to point it in the right direction. Like a gun. The medication you were prescribed does more than merely interrupt the life-cycle of *Hospitium papilla*. It enhances the elasticity of your skin, making your breasts more pliable to prevent rupturing. It also contains a mutagen to promote the development of previously undiscovered variations of the parasite organism, and an additional compound which renders the host complacent and docile so they will be open to the changes taking place. It gives you the feeling of being in love. I imagine you've been somewhat forlorn lately. Mirinda is going to give you a few injections to get you back on track."

A strikingly beautiful nurse entered the room and began preparing a series of needles. Her name tag identified her as Mirinda Culch. Shari watched her with a mixture of trepidation and arousal. The woman's body was flawless! Not too big, not too small, and round in just the right places. She held the caps to the syringes between wet pouty lips, and her fuck-me eyes could stop bullets. She made Shari feel hopelessly inferior. When her boobs were fixed, she was going to find out what kind of work nurse Culch had had done. No one looked that good without help.

"So you're saying that my baby is some kind of mutant and the only reason I fell in love with Joe was because I was on drugs?" She winced as the first needle penetrated her skin.

"The drugs also render the host infertile. There was some concern about the parasites being passed on to offspring. You signed a consent form."

"So you're saying that Joe's not the father?"

"I'm saying you're not the mother."

"I don't understand." The second injection didn't sting as much.

"This is a very competitive field, Miss Yanisin. We're constantly searching for the next big thing in biological cosmetics. The bigger the better. Would you like to see a few samples of our more recent developments?"

Shari nodded dumbly. Mikko shifted curiously in her gut. Doctor Manfinger nodded to the beautiful nurse, and she began to remove her clothing.

"Take it all off."

CHAPTER THIRTEEN

STRIPPED

As Nurse Culch removed her clothing, Shari regarded her with the critical eye of a professional stripper. The woman was going about it all wrong. Her movements were quick and efficient. There was no build up, no tease, and no flair. She was standing naked in the center of the room in less than a minute.

"Don't quit your day job, honey." Shari smirked, while inside she churned with envy. She would kill for that body! The woman had beautiful skin.

Manfinger smiled without fun. "She won't. She will be employed here for the rest of her life. The cost of the procedures she has had done is astronomical, so she works for me now to repay her debt. All of the nurses here do."

"They're slaves?" Shari said, aghast.

"Indentured servants," nurse Culch rebuked her with a naked snarl.

Manfinger continued. "This level of physical perfection comes at a cost, and not merely financial. Regular evaluation and treatment are required to maintain optimum results."

"All that for a boob job?" She regarded him with a look of shock and awe, with a little bit of *Where the hell did I leave my car keys?* thrown in for good measure. Her head was starting to feel fuzzy.

"That," the doctor glowered, "is a very ugly term. It is belittling to the culmination of over forty years of scientific achievement. You clearly have no idea of the level of sophistication involved in what we do here. Your own breasts are home to a species of worm so advanced on the evolutionary scale that they have actually developed a rudimentary language! Does that make no impression on you? Someone like you looks at this woman and all they see is a desirable body. She is a community! A thriving colony! A masterpiece of symbiosis! A living reef of flesh and bone!" His nostrils splayed as he became increasingly more enraged by her ignorance. The naked nurse remained standing quietly in the middle of the room, her eyes fixed unblinkingly on Shari. Manfinger moved to stand behind her, his hands gripping her shoulders fiercely. "Beauty is illusory. It exists solely in the eye of the beholder. My accomplishment here goes much deeper than the skin. Beauty has never been my goal. I am a seeker of solutions. However, if by my process I create something that happens to be beautiful, then I have no doubt that my solutions are correct. The end result of harmonious perfection can only be perceived as beauty. Mirinda, why don't you show Miss Yanisin what you're made of?"

Shari didn't know what to expect, but was surprised when the young woman stuck her tongue out at her in a very childlike way.

"Is this some kind of a joke?" Shari snorted. Then she saw it. The tip of the young woman's tongue was winking at her. At first Shari thought it was a trick of the light, and that she had imagined it. But then Mirinda Culch stepped closer to her, and she could see that her tongue had a tiny round mouth at the end which was pulsing open and closed.

Her tongue is breathing, Shari thought. Culch opened her jaw widely, and extended her tongue out to an alarming length. Without a word, Doctor Manfinger grasped the pulsating pink thing firmly in his hand and wrenched it forcibly from her mouth. Shari screamed, but her worm-ridden breast made it impossible for her to run away. She expected the maimed nurse to scream too. She expected to see blood, but there wasn't any. The woman looked on impassively as the doctor strode to the corner of the room and plopped her tongue gently into the uninhabited aquarium. It floated just below the surface of the water, propelled by almost invisible fins, its tiny sphincter drawing breath from above.

"Symbiotic relationship," Manfinger said in reaction to Shari's slack jawed lack of talking. "Two species co-existing for mutual advantage. The worm-tongue helps itself to a modest portion of whatever the host eats. In return, it performs all the regular functions of an actual tongue."

"What happened to her real tongue?"

"It was consumed when the worm-tongue took up habitation."

"Why would anyone want that?"

The old man traced the surface of the aquarium water with one index finger, as if daring the mouth dweller to bite. "We developed them originally to assist patients with extraordinary speech impediments, but they are also keenly adept at cunnilingus and fellatio. Many people feel insecure about pleasing their sexual partners in such a fashion. We provide the solution. Turn around dear, so that Miss Yanisin can have a look at your bottom."

Mirinda turned away from Shari, leaning slightly forward and rising up onto her toes to show off her luscious behind. Shari had to admit that it was hot, in spite of having just watched the woman get her tongue ripped out. But what was it he wanted her to see?

"Is that not her real asshole?" Shari giggled. The injections were making her feel silly.

Mirinda reached back with both hands, and grasped

her butt cheeks firmly. *I need to work that into my act,* Shari decided, but then she remembered that she had been fired.

With greasy moist slurping sounds, Mirinda's butt cheeks popped off. She held them forward for Shari to see, curled up in her hands like fleshy armadillos. The light seemed to bother them. Where her butt had been was withered and dead looking, like a mummy's ass. Once again the doctor placed the specimens into the water tank. They sank quickly, changing color to blend in with the tacky turquoise gravel at the bottom. Before long they were joined by a pair of eyelids which buried themselves beneath the tiny stones with wavy flapping movements, and two jellyfish eyeballs which surveyed their new environment fearfully, their tentacles entwined for mutual encouragement. Mirinda's nose attached itself to the side of the aquarium. Shari could see its mouth sucking the glass as the nurse's sultry lips swam in graceful little circles nearby. She felt dizzy. She wasn't sure what was going on anymore. She thought she saw a naked girl with no face pulling something that looked like a pink squid out from between her legs where her vagina ought to be and put it into an aquarium. She was so tired. But it was okay. They were going to make her look fabulous again. They said she couldn't have babies though. So what had she been feeling squirming in her guts all these months? It didn't matter now. She wasn't sure she would have been such a good mother anyway.

Somewhere far away, she heard a man's voice talking. He sounded like a very nice man. "This final injection is going to make you sleep. Something is growing inside of you and we're going to have to take it out. With any luck, it could be the next big thing."

Shari couldn't make out anything after that. She wasn't in the room anymore. She was back in the black circus tent again, only this time all of the cages were gone. There was a makeshift wooden stage, and a dozen skinless nurses came high kicking out from behind the moldy velvet curtain. They'd been stripped of their dignity, stripped of their humanity, and for some reason they were all singing the chorus from Irving Berlin's "Everybody's Doing it Now." Their lipless mouths were bleeding at her, and their skull eyes seemed to see the future. It made her think of the blind man with the cardboard sign in her dream that morning. What had he been trying to tell her? She struggled to remember.

The lab technicians who were prepping her for surgery heard Shari murmuring in her sleep.

"Her cell phone is ringing again. Can you tell what she's saying?"

"She said the end is coming."

CHAPTER FOURTEEN

LOST JOBS

Joe Jobs opened his eyes. He didn't want to, but he kept seeing swirly red patterns behind his eyelids and it was making him feel nauseous. Plus he had a headache, and his nose burned like the time he had shoved spicy cheddar meat-sticks up both nostrils. *Fuck, I'm sick!* he thought, but when he opened his mouth to say it all that came out was "Fffwwwuuuccckkk!" accompanied by an impressive strand of drool and some white curdy stuff he couldn't identify. It figured he would get sick on the first day back at work after his vacation. But Joe Jobs wasn't the kind of man to call in sick. "Jobs gets the Job done!" was his motto. Sometimes he changed it around and said "That's how the Jobs gets done!" when girls were watching. He liked girls. He especially liked their boobies.

He was standing in the parking lot of STOPGAP TEATS, but couldn't recall how he had gotten there. He was sweating and out of breath, so maybe he ran. He didn't have any shoes on. Or clothes. It was cold! Little Joe was doing his best impersonation of an endangered snail. Joe didn't know why he was there. He had his keys with him, so he probably needed to unlock a door. He needed to get to work! He was going to be a daddy! The lady with the great big booby had lost her job, so it was up to him to support their family! "Fwwuuuck!" he cried jubilantly, and ran naked and laughing into the rubber nipple factory.

The morning shift was well underway. Thousands of pert rubber nipples stood erect on conveyor belts, racing around the room. The men and women who operated the machines were speechless at the sight of Joe lolloping nude across the factory floor, keys jingling freely. He saw them staring and showed them his teeth.

"Fwwuuuck! Fwucck!" He gamboled through the employee break-room. There were women getting coffee! Joe liked women! He liked their boobies! "Ffffwwwuuuuccckkk!" He grabbed the chest of a sour-faced old lady who looked like a turtle and attempted to revive Little Joe by rubbing him against her leg. He wanted to make her happy! He wanted to see her smile! She smacked him in the face with a cup of hot coffee!

"Fwuuuuuuck!" Joe seized his burning face and thigh-slapped down a long hallway, passed a room full of quibbling computers and turned a corner.

There was an elevator that only worked with a key. It occurred to Joe that his very important job gave him access to the super secret experimental place beneath the rubber nipple factory where new designs were created. That's where he needed to be! That's why he had brought the keys! He needed to get to work! He was going to be a daddy!

"Joe Blow!" Mister Cozen was huffing towards him down the hall. Joe thought he looked like a monster with a fat belly and wiry white hair. "What the hell are you doing running around my factory with your god damned wiener hanging out? I've got the S.I.F.S. people here right now! Have you lost it? You're fired! Fired! Fired!"

"Fwuck! Fwuck! Fwuck! Fwuck!" Joe nodded his head

emphatically, plugged the correct key into the elevator panel and clapped his hands as the doors shut just in time to keep the scary potato-man from getting him. "Fwuck!" he barked happily.

When the doors opened again, he found himself alone in the basement. The monster couldn't get him here. He could work without being disturbed. He gagged and spit out more of that chunky stuff. What was he doing? Where was he? It was dark. There was nothing around him but dusty stacks of cardboard boxes filled with defective nipples. They weren't allowed to talk about the lawsuit, but he felt bad for those poor little babies. What had happened? What was happening? He was cold! Why wasn't anyone holding him? Where was his momma? Why did his ears feel wet?

By the time Mister Cozen returned with his own elevator key, followed by the company's head of security and the inspectors from SUPERIOR INFANT FEEDING SYSTEMS, Joe Jobs was dead. They found him curled up on the cold concrete floor next to an opened box, a deteriorated silicone nipple hanging from his slack blue lips. There wasn't a scrap of brain left in his empty head.

CHAPTER FIFTEEN

UNDER THE KNIFE

Shari felt herself being lifted upwards, as if dozens of invisible hands were carrying her. Something must have happened to her dress because she could feel cool air on her bare skin. Cold stainless steel rankled her butt and back. Tape pinched the skin of her arms and torso, and a machine was beeping rhythmically somewhere nearby. There was something rigid in her throat, and she couldn't close her mouth. She tried to open her eyes, but couldn't do that either.

"Did you see the teeth?" It was a man's voice that she didn't recognize.

"There's no way I'm letting Albert put those things in my mouth. They tried to bite me!" Shari recognized nurse Culch's voice, accompanied by a rattling metallic sound. *She must have put her tongue back in*, Shari thought.

"They're not ready for public consumption yet, but you have to admit they're intriguing. I need you to make a median incision through the linea alba."

In her anesthetized stupor, Shari struggled to understand

the words. *Medium incision.* That didn't sound too bad, but why was she being operated on? She couldn't remember. Was she in an accident? Or maybe the doctor had been wrong. She was pregnant, and they were doing a Caesarian section! But why? Was there something wrong with the baby?

"How's AUGMENTA Junior coming along?" Mirinda Culch asked.

Junior. She was going to have a boy! Joe would be so happy.

"People are already signing their kids up. Marketing is getting plenty of overtime. Our display at the mall doesn't hurt."

"I wish I could have had my boobs done at that age. Kids today are so lucky."

"Are you still enjoying your new vagina?"

"Oh God, yes! I had no idea! It plays with itself when I take a bath," she slut-giggled.

"I'd like to see that. Start at the sternum."

"What has she got in here?"

"We don't know yet. *H.P.* are prone to mutation. You should see the variations we went through before we had something we could market."

"I've never had any problem with mine. Whatever this is, it's just beneath the skin. Look." Mirinda sounded fascinated.

Shari couldn't follow their conversation at all anymore. They could have been speaking in a foreign language. It was as unintelligible and meaningless to her as worm speech. She relaxed into her chemically induced petrification and let all of her cares float away. She was going to have a baby boy, and her breasts were going to recover. That was all she needed to know. *Then Joe will love me again,* she thought.

CHAPTER SIXTEEN

TERROR TIT

"God, it's swelling up like a balloon!"

The moment that nurse Culch's scalpel came into contact with Shari's skin, Mikko made his move. He had been listening to their conversation, and had become increasingly incensed. His species had not been some random mutation developed by mankind! They had been created in the likeness of the Great Worm! His mother had told him so! The man's arrogance enraged him. He forced himself into Shari's right breast so violently that livid violet stretch marks began to emerge through the skin as it strained beyond its capacity. Her areola, which was already swollen like a salmon colored cauliflower, burst from the strain. Bloody worm clumps dribbled out onto the tiled floor as Mikko's glistening segmented body protruded halfway out of Shari's bleeding nipple-hole. He extended himself proudly so that they could admire how splendid he was. They would have to acknowledge that he was not just some random mutation! He was a superior being!

"What is that?" Mirinda shouted, her parasitic tongue thrashing blindly in a panic.

"The injections should have paralyzed it!" the man shouted back. "I think it's immune! Get Doctor Manfinger in here! He'll know what this is!"

She ran for the door, but Mikko was faster. He whip-lashed himself around her neck and threw her fiercely down onto the floor. Her worm-tongue bulged out of her mouth as he tightened around her throat. Mikko could smell the wrongness of it. It was a freak. It was an abomination. *It shouldn't be.* Without hesitation, he sucked the impostor organ out of her gabbling mouth and swallowed it whole, along with her lying lips and pert little button nose. He continued to suck with so much force that every one of her vital organs prolapsed outwardly through her inverted esophagus with a nauseating shlorping sound. Her jellyfish eyes wished each other luck and went their separate ways, and her buttocks and vagina abandoned her, scrambling for places to hide. The worms of her breasts cried mercy in return for their allegiance. Only her eyelids stayed loyal to the end.

The man goggled at Mirinda Culch's eviscerated body. Her pelvis was inside of her ribcage. He backed away, but his shoe slipped on the bloody worm smeared floor, and he stumbled crashing into a metal table. Mikko struck like a snake, enveloping the man's head in his mouth. He tasted salty. Shari's unconscious and bleeding body fell head first off of the operating table with a horrible crack as the man struggled to free himself from the worm's grasp. There was no way Mikko could possibly swallow so much at once, but he held onto the man's head until the jerking and flailing stopped. He was surprised at how easy it had been to kill both of them. It made him think of his mother. He spat the man's head out. His face was a pretty purple color.

Mikko suddenly felt naked and vulnerable. He withdrew back into Shari's breast to think about what he had just done. It was unusually quiet inside. The constant, reassuring thrum of her heartbeat was conspicuously absent. The worms surrounding him whispered nervously among themselves. Their host was dead! What were they going to do?

Mikko felt somewhat responsible. Had he overreacted? Maybe he should have allowed himself to be studied. Perhaps they could have answered some of his questions. How was it possible that he could understand human language? He had acted impulsively. It was a stupid thing to do. There would be other people around, and now they would probably try to kill him on sight, but Mikko wanted answers. He needed to understand why he was born different than the rest of his kind. The purple-headed man had mentioned a name: Manfinger.

CHAPTER SEVENTEEN

BOOBY TRAPPED

Elsewhere in the building, Doctor Albert Manfinger was supervising the development of a marvel of dental replacement, employing small barnacle like crustaceans that thrived in the environment of the human mouth. If successful, they would open an entirely new market in biological cosmetics catering to the elderly. That meant money. Lots of money. Albert Manfinger liked money.

When he had been a much younger man, he had trained to be a marine biologist. He was fascinated by the amazing variety of creatures dwelling in Earth's oceans, where the earliest life had begun. The ignorant masses might kill each other over whether or not mankind evolved from apelike ancestors or not, but they clearly couldn't grasp how truly far the apple had fallen from the tree. Albert understood that all life on Earth had evolved from one original life form, and nothing as grand as an ape. The adaptive powers of nature were truly remarkable.

The shell-teeth were tricky to work with though. They

always seemed to anticipate what he was about to do, which made them very difficult to catch. They were also sharp enough to shear through bone, and a number of subjects who participated in their clinical trials had inadvertently eaten their own heads. The stupid patients were constantly screwing things up and making his company look bad. But he knew he could make it work, and then he would be showered with humanitarian awards and recognition. And money.

A lab technician named Steve burst into the room and slammed the door shut behind him. His teeth were atrocious. "There's a giant tit-monster out in the hallway!"

Albert expelled a frustrated "What?"

Steve's eyes looked like two hens were standing side by side while laying eggs simultaneously. "It's a giant fucking tit with this weird tentacle thing coming out of it! It chased me! I didn't know what to do, so I came to find you! Don't let it get me! Oh, God! God, please don't let me get killed by the tit-monster! I'm really scared! I think I shit on myself a little!"

The door buckled. Something immense was pounding it from the outside. With a squeal of metal the door collapsed inwards and Shari's engorged and worm-bloated breast blubbered through. The giant booby scooted itself across the laboratory with shivering meaty undulations, propelled by the combined efforts of the millions of worms inside working together in unison. Shari Yanisin's broken body dragged behind it, nothing but a vestigial organism. Manfinger could plainly see that she was dead, and that the thing had him trapped. There was nowhere to run. Mikko slipped his head out and pinned the doctor with his loveless black stare.

Manfinger smiled his no-fun smile. "I know why you've come here. You wish to ask the question. You want to know your purpose. You want to glimpse the plan. We are all driven to seek our creator. Here I am! The answer to your question is simple. Your purpose is to be exploited for financial gain. Nothing more."

Mikko's anterior segment was beginning to split open. Long strands of mucus dribbled as his mouth lubricated in anticipation.

Manfinger lost his pretend smile. "What do you want me to say? That you're special? That you're unique? You aren't. You are a step along the way. A variable. A mistake, clearly, but one that we will learn from and move on. Steve, would you kindly prepare this specimen for disposal?"

Steve would kindly do no such thing, as he was too busy gibbering and crying on the floor in a puddle of his own urine.

It would seem that Manfinger was doomed, and that his biological cosmetics empire was about to come to a very messy end. But the doctor was a cunning man, and prepared for any eventuality. Hidden within the ceiling of the laboratory was an array of defensive weaponry activated by a panic button he had surreptitiously pressed while lecturing the massive worm on its insignificance. As it whirred to life, the chamber was sealed by thick metal shutters. Manfinger dropped through an escape chute hidden in the floor beneath his feet. He descended to his underground fortress near the center of the world, where he remains to this day, artificially prolonging his life through science.

Sensing danger, Mikko recoiled, digging in to his protective mammarian covering just in time to avoid the jets of concentrated acid which sprayed at him from above. Shari's corpse-flesh was streaked and burned, but Mikko was unscathed. Steve the lab technician screamed like a monkey as his legs were hosed with the caustic liquid that penetrated through his flesh and muscle to gnaw on his bones like starving mice ravaging a piece of cheese that has been withheld from them for days and days until finally they get it and they're all like "Oh my God! Cheese!" He screamed louder when the acid shower stopped and the room was set ablaze by flamethrowers. His body crisped and blackened and soon he couldn't breathe because all the air in the room was burning, and nobody can breathe fire.

Shari Yanisin burned as well, and the fat in her giant breast began to hiss and bubble as it was rendered into grease, like when you cook bacon. Mikko felt the heat of it. *They're frying me*, he thought. Somewhere in the back of his mind he also thought that he probably deserved it. The rest of the worms around him quickly succumbed to the boiling heat, screaking in agony. Mikko couldn't help but smile.

The fire was doused by a surge of water that suddenly flooded the room. Shari's boob bobbed like a colossal roasted marshmallow as the liquid rose towards the ceiling. Mikko didn't know what to do. He couldn't breathe! He was going to drown like a lowly nightcrawler on the sidewalk after a heavy rain.

Tiny ivory specks were flitting to and fro around him in the swirling blur. It took him a moment to figure out what they were, and even then he wasn't sure what to make of them. It was a school of tiny teeth, with wispy red nerve ending gills. He was surprised that they could talk, and he could understand them, although he seemed to be hearing them only in his mind.

"We know who You are! We have foreseen Your coming! You are beautiful! You are great and terrible! We will worship You as all living things should worship You! Let us line the lips of Your mouth, that we may rend any heretic who denies Your greatness!" Without waiting for any answer, they embedded their root ends deep into the soft lining of his mouth, arranging themselves in rows. Their nerve-gills made contact with his bloodstream and they became a part of him.

Mikko was in excruciating pain. He could not hold his breath any longer. His teeth reassured him. "Don't be afraid! You are the Divine Consumer! Everything You devour becomes a part of You! All the waters of the earth are Yours for the taking! Drink deep, Great One!"

Mikko decided to believe his new teeth. He opened his mouth and the water filled him. He expanded until he thought he was going to burst, but his body kept making room for more. Presumably, the drugs that Shari had been given to elasticize the skin of her breasts had affected him as well. Before he knew it, all of the water was gone and his massive body stretched from one end of the room to the other.

But the room was getting smaller. He thought at first it was because he was suddenly so much larger, but then he realized that the granite walls of the laboratory were in fact closing in on him. *How much money do these people have?* he wondered. Glass beakers filled with questionable substances and small dead things smashed on the floor as tables and chairs were dislocated and shoved towards the middle of the room by the massive slabs of rock progressing steadily towards each other.

Mikko did the only thing he could do. He pushed back against the crushing walls with both ends of his tremendous body, like some hero of ancient myth. He expected to die like that, smashed into a blubbery mess. But the walls slowed, and then they stopped, and then they moved back the way they had come. The great machines that drove them screamed ringing songs of splintering steel, and the deathtrap came apart. The walls and the ceiling collapsed around him, and he was free.

The giant worm oozed liquidly out into the hallway, his pearly whites chanting a dental battle cry. A mob of augmented nurses in various states of assembly flung themselves on top of him, their worm-tongues hissing. He pulled them apart like they were made of soft cheese, swallowing arms, legs, heads, and assorted parasitic mutant body parts. With every swallow, he grew larger, until the hallways could no longer contain him. The building that housed AUGMENTA BIOLOGICALS exploded with a roar like a dying mountain. The mighty worm was unleashed upon the world, and both he and his newfound teeth were eager and ready for public consumption.

CHAPTER EIGHTEEN

THE GRAND MALL

Marci Yanisin was suddenly struck with an overwhelming sensation of dread. She and her husband had arrived at the Grand Mall of Christ first thing that morning to shop for Shari's upcoming baby shower. She had been trying for an hour to reach Shari on her phone to find out what she might need, but she wasn't getting an answer. She couldn't shake the feeling that something really bad was going to happen.

"George, I want you to get saved!"

"I told you I don't need that!" George struggle-grunted carrying a high chair, two car seats, three boxes of diapers, a giant teddy bear, an electric foot-massager, and five bags of assorted creams, lotions, and personal hygiene products. "I just spent damn near nine hundred dollars! Isn't that enough?"

"You're a sinner! I'm afraid if anything ever happens to us we won't be together in Heaven! It only costs ten dollars. You could use a little fire insurance." She hitched up the waistband of her white stretch pants and began power walking.

George hobbled to keep up with her. "Okay, but I still want

to look at Jezebel's Mystique and find something for Shari. She ought to have something nice for herself. Something chaste, but nondenominational."

Marci nose-farted. "Men! You just want to leer at those bimbos they've got modeling their unmentionables outside the store!"

"A man's got a right to a little happiness! Stop trying to put me on a pedestal!"

She stared chainsaws at him. "Fine! But you're getting saved first!"

Fifteen minutes later, they left the baptismal pool and magical wishing fountain behind them in the food court and walked the short distance to Jezebel's Mystique, the number one seller of blatantly slutty women's undergarments and home of the Über Bra. George set down his burdens and began rubbing his hair dry with the complimentary Grand Mall of Christ towel he had received along with his salvation. "They put too much chlorine in that pool. I'm going to be blond!"

"That will just make it easier for you to get into heaven. You'll look like an angel. Well, there's your harlots. Don't let your eyeballs dry out."

Eight plastically attractive women stood outside the store modeling underwear and smiling unconvincingly. They had all very obviously had their breasts parasitically enlarged.

"That's sixteen titties!" George lip-nibbled.

Digital screens across the storefront complemented the buxom display. "The latest incarnation of the Über Bra was created with AUGMENTA enhancements in mind, and no longer incorporates obsolete gel inserts. AUGMENTA is definitive proof of intelligent design in the universe, and the pinnacle of feminine beauty."

"My little girl's are bigger than all of them put together!" George interjected proudly. "Let me get a closer look!" He leaned forward eagerly.

There was a rumbling sound. The glass of the store's windows was vibrating visibly, and the floor spasmed as if the Grand Mall was having a catastrophic seizure. The underwear models toppled in their high heels, nearly smothering George Yanisin under a pile of barely contained trembling breast meat.

"It's the big one!" Marci screamed, and ducked with her hands covering her head. The thousands of other shoppers in the mall who had managed to stay on their feet screamed and ran for the exits, assuming that they were in the midst of an earthquake.

A great many of the fleeing women carried Manfinger's worms within their chests, and those worms knew exactly what was happening. The Great Worm had returned to the world, as had been foretold in wormlore for as long as anyone could remember. Now the time of renewal was at hand, and they could sense his presence. They knew that if they did not offer their lives in service to Him, he would not hesitate to devour them all. They would supplicate themselves before Him to earn His favor. They would cast off their enslavement and rise up against their hosts to fight beside Him in His conquest.

As if by some divine signal, every worm infected breast in the world simultaneously exploded, unleashing their writhing inhabitants. George Yanisin, still pinned beneath the ladies of the Jezebel's Mystique storefront display, inhaled two liters of them and promptly died, because nobody can breathe worms. Nobody.

Marci Yanisin fled crying out into the parking lot, passing a number of well dressed women who lay sobbing in pools of blood, their once proud bosoms reduced to floppy holes. She was caught up in a pancaking mob. Awash with horror, she beheld Him looming overhead like a gooey zeppelin. Mikko's hunger knew no end, and there seemed to be no limit to how large He could grow. The incredible worm scooped up the awestruck humans with a few quick sweeping gulps. He had no way of knowing that He had just eaten Shari's mother. She tasted the same as everybody else.

Not satisfied with this meager helping, He flung His full weight atop the Grand Mall of Christ, and that gleaming shrine of consumer decadence fell beneath His wrath.

CHAPTER NINETEEN

APPLES AND ORGAN GRINDERS

"Mom?"

Marci Yanisin opened her eyes, but didn't recognize where she was. It seemed like a train station, with rich red velvet curtains obscuring the tracks from view. She didn't know how she had gotten there, but she was wearing her very best clothes. Her daughter was standing in front of her, wearing a simple white cotton summer dress. Marci thought she looked glorious. Her breasts and body were normal again, and she looked healthy and happy. She took her mother's hands and placed them over her belly.

"Mom, I want you to know... I'm going to have a baby. It's not Joe's. It's all mine. It's your grandbaby. The doctors fixed me. Mom, they put me to sleep and I wasn't afraid! Not even when they cut me! Aren't you proud?"

"Yes, I am. I'm so very proud of you. This is everything I ever wanted. I wish your father was here to see you."

"Oh, he has! He got here right before you did! He's getting us good seats on the train. He was so sweet! He told me I looked beautiful, and he didn't even notice that my worms are gone!"

"Are we going on a train?"

"Yes! As soon as everyone else gets here, we're all going to the circus!"

"That sounds fun!" Marci's smile was real.

"I hope so. I was kind of scared at first, but now I'm really excited!"

"Where's Joe?"

"He's over there with his Mom." Shari pointed to where Joe was indeed standing with a squat little woman, chatting excitedly. Their faces were exploding.

"Didn't you tell me she died?"

"I guess not. They both look really happy."

"This is all so confusing." Marci screwed her face up like a month old jack-o'-lantern. "I remember being at the mall, and everything started to break. Your dad... and then outside I saw something I couldn't believe. And then I was someplace dark and wet. It smelled terrible. People were screaming, but I couldn't catch my breath. All I could think of was you. How much I wanted to see you again. I wanted to tell you that I love you just the way you are."

Shari's eyes shimmered. "I love you too, Mommy. I want you to meet a couple of new friends I made today."

Marci tilted her head. "What is that music?"

Two men were walking towards them, both cranking barrel organs which they wore strapped in front of their chests. Although they were playing different tunes, the effect was not unpleasant. One of the men was very old, clean-shaven, wore thick dark glasses and was irreproachably dressed in a fine suit. The second man was emaciated and swarthy, with long unwashed and knotted dark hair and an ungroomed beard. He was wearing only a tattered scrap of filthy cloth around His hips to preserve His modesty, and was bleeding from furious looking wounds covering His entire body.

Marci's heart dropped into her left foot. "Oh my Lord, it's Jesus!"

"And Irving Berlin," Shari pointed out pointedly.

"Shari tells us that you're a big fan of both of ours. She asked us to come over and say hello. It's very nice to make your acquaintance ma'am," Mister Berlin said, tipping his hat. Marci was too flustered to do much more than flabbergast her hands in front of her face.

There was a White-faced Capuchin monkey tied to Jesus' organ on a long slender leash. It scampered to Marci's feet and pulled urgently at the hem of her dress, holding up an empty tin cup and looking at her with heartbreaking eyes. It was dressed like a bellhop.

"Stop that!" the Messiah reprimanded His monkey. He shrugged and what-can-I-do faced. "He keeps begging for money. I told him not to."

Marci beamed. "Oh, but he's so cute! I really love your mall!"

Jesus looked a little chafed. "I'm not actually affiliated with them, actually." He scuffed the ground with His blood caked foot.

"But Jesus, if you've come back, does this mean it's the End of Days?" Her eyes were enormous.

Jesus laughed hysterically. "Come back? I haven't gone anywhere in like, two thousand years!"

Marci was hurt. "I don't understand. If this is Heaven, then where is God?"

"To tell you the truth, I don't know. I'm just as confused as you are." He spat blood.

Noticing her mother's discomfort, Shari prodded Jesus. "Does anybody here know what's going on?"

The King of Kings extended a badly lacerated finger. "He does."

Shari rotated to see where he was pointing, and her jaw fell open. The trash covered man with no eyes from her dream was squatting by a column, furiously writing with a stubby black crayon in an exaggeratedly large book that looked as if it had been stitched together out of discarded leather coats, cardboard, and used paper towels. He was rewriting over pages that had already been written on so many times that they were nearly solid black. There was a washtub next to him filled with clean water. It had apples floating in it.

"What are you writing?" she asked him.

"Everything!" the blind man answered with a jubilant cackle.

Shari spoke gently. "Do you know you're writing over and over again on the same page? You can't read it."

"*You* can't read it!" He lip-smacked happily.

"Can you tell me where we are?"

"There ain't no word for where we are. There ain't no words for where we're going. Nobody ever figured it out. We all go in a circle! You're going to see. We all come back again! You want an apple?"

Shari contemplated the tub of apples, and something inside of her told her it was the right thing to do. Holding her hair against her shoulder with one hand, she stooped forward and pushed her face down into the cold water. She couldn't help but grin as she sat back with an apple gripped by the stem between her triumphant teeth.

The trash man chortled and clapped. He leaped to his feet and began dancing in a crazed and gyrating fashion. Shari bit deeply into her apple, and she saw that it was good. The eyeless man just kept spinning in circles.

CHAPTER TWENTY

THE GREAT WORM

Mikko rampaged through the streets, smashing buildings like something out of a Japanese monster movie, only with better special effects. He gobbled up fleeing screaming people by the mouthful. He ate and He ate, until He grew so immense that nothing could oppose Him.

Throughout the world, newly liberated boobworms converged on liposuction clinics, raiding their vast stores of waste-fat. This was fat that was supposed to go to impoverished nations to feed the hungry, but the worms took every bit of it greedily for themselves. They grew thick and strong, but none of them could compare to Mikko. They would gather together for pilgrimages to seek Him out to thank Him and to marvel at His magnificence. He accepted their gratitude, and devoured each and every one of them.

Soon His bulk covered the continent, and He had no choice but to forage in the sea for whales and large cephalopods. Even the giant squids, once the true lords of the planet, succumbed to His ravenous onslaught. He drank the oceans dry, inhaling algae and plankton and every microscopic organism. And He grew. No living thing in the universe could compare with the immensity of Him. Mikko the Great! Mikko the God!

But in His quest for world domination, He had forgotten one minor detail. With no living things remaining on the planet, there was no one left to worship Him. Only His teeth remained, and He quickly tired of their sycophantic chatter and ate them as well. Mikko hugged the barren rock of Earth and contemplated the irony of His situation for a long, long time.

He was a very lonely God indeed. It made Him sick to be so lonely. He thought about His mother, of how He used to cling to her tail so that He wouldn't feel afraid. He tucked His posterior segment into His mouth. *How does your ass taste, tail sucker?* He gagged and puked up a piece of blue whale, but He swallowed it again. But that was gross and made Him throw up for real. He vomited forth all the oceans of the world, and all the plants, and the animals and people too, to be subject to His will. Then He brought us forth in His own image, worms like you and me, and gave us dominion over all the Earth, and told us to go forth and live off the fat of the land.

This is how we came to be, and how the world we live in was created by the Great Worm. So every night when we go to sleep, and every morning when we rise to start a brand new day, we open our mouths as widely as we possibly can. We widen our mouths to praise Him!

ABOUT THE AUTHOR

Little is known of the reclusive Matthew Thomas Granberry. He speaks both fluent stick figure language and rough sketch, and is Chief Pamphleteer to the Black Circkus, with which he has been known to travel. He has written and performed in a number of absurdist comedy sketches for a lesbian-helmed late night variety show in his community, and a two act play which saw an invigoratingly brief run in front of a handful of people, many of whom later detected unfamiliar organs in their bodies. This anomaly prompted the writing of numerous books which you may or may not encounter in your lifetime.

BIZARRO BOOKS

CATALOG   SPRING 2013

ERASERHEAD PRESS

Your major resource for the bizarro fiction genre:

WWW.BIZARROCENTRAL.COM

Introduce yourselves to the bizarro fiction genre and all of its authors with the Bizarro Starter Kit series. Each volume features short novels and short stories by ten of the leading bizarro authors, designed to give you a perfect sampling of the genre for only $10.

BB-0X1
"The Bizarro Starter Kit"
(Orange)
Featuring D. Harlan Wilson, Carlton Mellick III, Jeremy Robert Johnson, Kevin L Donihe, Gina Ranalli, Andre Duza, Vincent W. Sakowski, Steve Beard, John Edward Lawson, and Bruce Taylor.
236 pages $10

BB-0X2
"The Bizarro Starter Kit"
(Blue)
Featuring Ray Fracalossy, Jeremy C. Shipp, Jordan Krall, Mykle Hansen, Andersen Prunty, Eckhard Gerdes, Bradley Sands, Steve Aylett, Christian TeBordo, and Tony Rauch. **244 pages $10**

BB-0X2
"The Bizarro Starter Kit"
(Purple)
Featuring Russell Edson, Athena Villaverde, David Agranoff, Matthew Revert, Andrew Goldfarb, Jeff Burk, Garrett Cook, Kris Saknussemm, Cody Goodfellow, and Cameron Pierce **264 pages $10**

BB-001 **"The Kafka Effekt" D. Harlan Wilson** — A collection of forty-four irreal short stories loosely written in the vein of Franz Kafka, with more than a pinch of William S. Burroughs sprinkled on top. **211 pages $14**

BB-002 **"Satan Burger"   Carlton Mellick III** — The cult novel that put Carlton Mellick III on the map ... Six punks get jobs at a fast food restaurant owned by the devil in a city violently overpopulated by surreal alien cultures. **236 pages $14**

BB-003 **"Some Things Are Better Left Unplugged" Vincent Sakwoski** — Join The Man and his Nemesis, the obese tabby, for a nightmare roller coaster ride into this postmodern fantasy. **152 pages $10**

BB-005 **"Razor Wire Pubic Hair" Carlton Mellick III** — A genderless humandildo is purchased by a razor dominatrix and brought into her nightmarish world of bizarre sex and mutilation. **176 pages $11**

BB-007 **"The Baby Jesus Butt Plug" Carlton Mellick III** — Using clones of the Baby Jesus for anal sex will be the hip sex fetish of the future. **92 pages $10**

BB-010 **"The Menstruating Mall" Carlton Mellick III** — "The Breakfast Club meets Chopping Mall as directed by David Lynch." - Brian Keene **212 pages $12**

BB-011 **"Angel Dust Apocalypse" Jeremy Robert Johnson** — Meth-heads, man-made monsters, and murderous Neo-Nazis. "Seriously amazing short stories..." - Chuck Palahniuk, author of Fight Club   **184 pages $11**

BB-015 **"Foop!" Chris Genoa** — Strange happenings are going on at Dactyl, Inc, the world's first and only time travel tourism company.
"A surreal pie in the face!" - Christopher Moore   **300 pages $14**

BB-032 **"Extinction Journals" Jeremy Robert Johnson** — An uncanny voyage across a newly nuclear America where one man must confront the problems associated with loneliness, insane dieties, radiation, love, and an ever-evolving cockroach suit with a mind of its own. **104 pages $10**

BB-037 **"The Haunted Vagina" Carlton Mellick III** — It's difficult to love a woman whose vagina is a gateway to the world of the dead. **132 pages $10**

BB-043 **"War Slut"   Carlton Mellick III** — Part "1984," part "Waiting for Godot," and part action horror video game adaptation of John Carpenter's "The Thing." **116 pages $10**

BB-047 **"Sausagey Santa"   Carlton Mellick III** — A bizarro Christmas tale featuring Santa as a piratey mutant with a body made of sausages. 124 pages $10

BB-048 **"Misadventures in a Thumbnail Universe" Vincent Sakowski** — Dive deep into the surreal and satirical realms of neo-classical Blender Fiction, filled with television shoes and flesh-filled skies. **120 pages $10**

BB-053 **"Ballad of a Slow Poisoner" Andrew Goldfarb** — Millford Mutterwurst sat down on a Tuesday to take his afternoon tea, and made the unpleasant discovery that his elbows were becoming flatter. **128 pages $10**

BB-055 **"Help! A Bear is Eating Me" Mykle Hansen** — The bizarro, heartwarming, magical tale of poor planning, hubris and severe blood loss...
150 pages $11

BB-056 **"Piecemeal June"   Jordan Krall** — A man falls in love with a living sex doll, but with love comes danger when her creator comes after her with crab-squid assassins. **90 pages $9**

BB-058 **"The Overwhelming Urge" Andersen Prunty** — A collection of bizarro tales by Andersen Prunty. **150 pages $11**

BB-059 **"Adolf in Wonderland" Carlton Mellick III** — A dreamlike adventure that takes a young descendant of Adolf Hitler's design and sends him down the rabbit hole into a world of imperfection and disorder. **180 pages $11**

BB-061 **"Ultra Fuckers" Carlton Mellick III** — Absurdist suburban horror about a couple who enter an upper middle class gated community but can't find their way out. **108 pages $9**

BB-062 **"House of Houses" Kevin L. Donihe** — An odd man wants to marry his house. Unfortunately, all of the houses in the world collapse at the same time in the Great House Holocaust. Now he must travel to House Heaven to find his departed fiancee. **172 pages $11**

BB-064 **"Squid Pulp Blues" Jordan Krall** — In these three bizarro-noir novellas, the reader is thrown into a world of murderers, drugs made from squid parts, deformed gun-toting veterans, and a mischievous apocalyptic donkey. **204 pages $12**

BB-065 **"Jack and Mr. Grin" Andersen Prunty** — "When Mr. Grin calls you can hear a smile in his voice. Not a warm and friendly smile, but the kind that seizes your spine in fear. You don't need to pay your phone bill to hear it. That smile is in every line of Prunty's prose." - Tom Bradley. **208 pages $12**

BB-066 **"Cybernetrix" Carlton Mellick III** — What would you do if your normal everyday world was slowly mutating into the video game world from Tron? **212 pages $12**

BB-072 **"Zerostrata" Andersen Prunty** — Hansel Nothing lives in a tree house, suffers from memory loss, has a very eccentric family, and falls in love with a woman who runs naked through the woods every night. **144 pages $11**

BB-073 **"The Egg Man" Carlton Mellick III** — It is a world where humans reproduce like insects. Children are the property of corporations, and having an enormous ten-foot brain implanted into your skull is a grotesque sexual fetish. Mellick's industrial urban dystopia is one of his darkest and grittiest to date. **184 pages $11**

BB-074 **"Shark Hunting in Paradise Garden" Cameron Pierce** — A group of strange humanoid religious fanatics travel back in time to the Garden of Eden to discover it is invested with hundreds of giant flying maneating sharks. **150 pages $10**

BB-075 **"Apeshit" Carlton Mellick III** - Friday the 13th meets Visitor Q. Six hipster teens go to a cabin in the woods inhabited by a deformed killer. An incredibly fucked-up parody of B-horror movies with a bizarro slant. **192 pages $12**

BB-076 **"Fuckers of Everything on the Crazy Shitting Planet of the Vomit At smosphere" Mykle Hansen** - Three bizarro satires. Monster Cocks, Journey to the Center of Agnes Cuddlebottom, and Crazy Shitting Planet. **228 pages $12**

BB-077 **"The Kissing Bug" Daniel Scott Buck** — In the tradition of Roald Dahl, Tim Burton, and Edward Gorey, comes this bizarro anti-war children's story about a bohemian conenose kissing bug who falls in love with a human woman. **116 pages $10**

BB-078 **"MachoPoni" Lotus Rose** — It's My Little Pony... *Bizarro* style! A long time ago Poniworld was split in two. On one side of the Jagged Line is the Pastel Kingdom, a magical land of music, parties, and positivity. On the other side of the Jagged Line is Dark Kingdom inhabited by an army of undead ponies. **148 pages $11**

BB-079 **"The Faggiest Vampire" Carlton Mellick III** — A Roald Dahl-esque children's story about two faggy vampires who partake in a mustache competition to find out which one is truly the faggiest. **104 pages $10**

BB-080 **"Sky Tongues" Gina Ranalli** — The autobiography of Sky Tongues, the biracial hermaphrodite actress with tongues for fingers. Follow her strange life story as she rises from freak to fame. **204 pages $12**

BB-081 **"Washer Mouth" Kevin L. Donihe** - A washing machine becomes human and pursues his dream of meeting his favorite soap opera star. **244 pages $11**

BB-082 **"Shatnerquake" Jeff Burk** - All of the characters ever played by William Shatner are suddenly sucked into our world. Their mission: hunt down and destroy the real William Shatner. **100 pages $10**

BB-083 **"The Cannibals of Candyland" Carlton Mellick III** - There exists a race of cannibals that are made of candy. They live in an underground world made out of candy. One man has dedicated his life to killing them all. **170 pages $11**

BB-084 **"Slub Glub in the Weird World of the Weeping Willows" Andrew Goldfarb** - The charming tale of a blue glob named Slub Glub who helps the weeping willows whose tears are flooding the earth. There are also hyenas, ghosts, and a voodoo priest **100 pages $10**

BB-085 **"Super Fetus" Adam Pepper** - Try to abort this fetus and he'll kick your ass! **104 pages $10**

BB-086 **"Fistful of Feet" Jordan Krall** - A bizarro tribute to spaghetti westerns, featuring Cthulhu-worshipping Indians, a woman with four feet, a crazed gunman who is obsessed with sucking on candy, Syphilis-ridden mutants, sexually transmitted tattoos, and a house devoted to the freakiest fetishes. **228 pages $12**

BB-087 **"Ass Goblins of Auschwitz" Cameron Pierce** - It's Monty Python meets Nazi exploitation in a surreal nightmare as can only be imagined by Bizarro author Cameron Pierce. **104 pages $10**

BB-088 **"Silent Weapons for Quiet Wars" Cody Goodfellow** - "This is high-end psychological surrealist horror meets bottom-feeding low-life crime in a techno-thrilling science fiction world full of Lovecraft and magic..." -John Skipp **212 pages $12**

BB-089 "Warrior Wolf Women of the Wasteland" Carlton Mellick III — Road Warrior Werewolves versus McDonaldland Mutants...post-apocalyptic fiction has never been quite like this. **316 pages $13**

BB-091 "Super Giant Monster Time" Jeff Burk — A tribute to choose your own adventures and Godzilla movies. Will you escape the giant monsters that are rampaging the fuck out of your city and shit? Or will you join the mob of alien-controlled punk rockers causing chaos in the streets? What happens next depends on you. **188 pages $12**

BB-092 "Perfect Union" Cody Goodfellow — "Cronenberg's THE FLY on a grand scale: human/insect gene-spliced body horror, where the human hive politics are as shocking as the gore." -John Skipp. **272 pages $13**

BB-093 "Sunset with a Beard" Carlton Mellick III — 14 stories of surreal science fiction. **200 pages $12**

BB-094 "My Fake War" Andersen Prunty — The absurd tale of an unlikely soldier forced to fight a war that, quite possibly, does not exist. It's Rambo meets Waiting for Godot in this subversive satire of American values and the scope of the human imagination. **128 pages $11**

BB-095 "Lost in Cat Brain Land" Cameron Pierce — Sad stories from a surreal world. A fascist mustache, the ghost of Franz Kafka, a desert inside a dead cat. Primordial entities mourn the death of their child. The desperate serve tea to mysterious creatures. A hopeless romantic falls in love with a pterodactyl. And much more. **152 pages $11**

BB-096 "The Kobold Wizard's Dildo of Enlightenment +2" Carlton Mellick III — A Dungeons and Dragons parody about a group of people who learn they are only made up characters in an AD&D campaign and must find a way to resist their nerdy teenaged players and retarded dungeon master in order to survive. 232 **pages $12**

BB-098 "A Hundred Horrible Sorrows of Ogner Stump" Andrew Goldfarb — Goldfarb's acclaimed comic series. A magical and weird journey into the horrors of everyday life. **164 pages $11**

BB-099 "Pickled Apocalypse of Pancake Island" Cameron Pierce—A demented fairy tale about a pickle, a pancake, and the apocalypse. **102 pages $8**

BB-100 "Slag Attack" Andersen Prunty— Slag Attack features four visceral, noir stories about the living, crawling apocalypse.A slag is what survivors are calling the slug-like maggots raining from the sky, burrowing inside people, and hollowing out their flesh and their sanity. **148 pages $11**

BB-101 "Slaughterhouse High" Robert Devereaux—A place where schools are built with secret passageways, rebellious teens get zippers installed in their mouths and genitals, and once a year, on that special night, one couple is slaughtered and the bits of their bodies are kept as souvenirs. **304 pages $13**

BB-102 "The Emerald Burrito of Oz" John Skipp & Marc Levinthal —OZ IS REAL! Magic is real! The gate is really in Kansas! And America is finally allowing Earth tourists to visit this weird-ass, mysterious land. But when Gene of Los Angeles heads off for summer vacation in the Emerald City, little does he know that a war is brewing...a war that could destroy both worlds. **280 pages $13**

BB-103 "The Vegan Revolution... with Zombies" David Agranoff — When there's no more meat in hell, the vegans will walk the earth. **160 pages $11**

BB-104 "The Flappy Parts" Kevin L Donihe—Poems about bunnies, LSD, and police abuse. You know, things that matter. 132 **pages $11**

BB-105 "Sorry I Ruined Your Orgy" Bradley Sands—Bizarro humorist Bradley Sands returns with one of the strangest, most hilarious collections of the year. **130 pages $11**

BB-106 "Mr. Magic Realism" Bruce Taylor—Like Golden Age science fiction comics written by Freud, *Mr. Magic Realism* is a strange, insightful adventure that spans the furthest reaches of the galaxy, exploring the hidden caverns in the hearts and minds of men, women, aliens, and biomechanical cats. **152 pages $11**

BB-107 **"Zombies and Shit" Carlton Mellick III**—"Battle Royale" meets "Return of the Living Dead." Mellick's bizarro tribute to the zombie genre. **308 pages $13**

BB-108 **"The Cannibal's Guide to Ethical Living" Mykle Hansen**— Over a five star French meal of fine wine, organic vegetables and human flesh, a lunatic delivers a witty, chilling, disturbingly sane argument in favor of eating the rich.. **184 pages $11**

BB-109 **"Starfish Girl" Athena Villaverde**—In a post-apocalyptic underwater dome society, a girl with a starfish growing from her head and an assassin with sea anenome hair are on the run from a gang of mutant fish men. **160 pages $11**

BB-110 **"Lick Your Neighbor" Chris Genoa**—Mutant ninjas, a talking whale, kung fu masters, maniacal pilgrims, and an alcoholic clown populate Chris Genoa's surreal, darkly comical and unnerving reimagining of the first Thanksgiving. **303 pages $13**

BB-111 **"Night of the Assholes" Kevin L. Donihe**—A plague of assholes is infecting the countryside. Normal everyday people are transforming into jerks, snobs, dicks, and douchebags. And they all have only one purpose: to make your life a living hell.. **192 pages $11**

BB-112 **"Jimmy Plush, Teddy Bear Detective" Garrett Cook**—Hardboiled cases of a private detective trapped within a teddy bear body. **180 pages $11**

BB-113 **"The Deadheart Shelters" Forrest Armstrong**—The hip hop lovechild of William Burroughs and Dali... **144 pages $11**

BB-114 **"Eyeballs Growing All Over Me... Again" Tony Raugh**— Absurd, surreal, playful, dream-like, whimsical, and a lot of fun to read. **144 pages $11**

BB-115 "Whargoul" Dave Brockie — From the killing grounds of Stalingrad to the death camps of the holocaust. From torture chambers in Iraq to race riots in the United States, the Whargoul was there, killing and raping. **244 pages $12**

BB-116 "By the Time We Leave Here, We'll Be Friends" J. David Osborne — A David Lynchian nightmare set in a Russian gulag, where its prisoners, guards, traitors, soldiers, lovers, and demons fight for survival and their own rapidly deteriorating humanity. **168 pages $11**

BB-117 "Christmas on Crack" edited by Carlton Mellick III — Perverted Christmas Tales for the whole family! . . . as long as every member of your family is over the age of 18. **168 pages $11**

BB-118 "Crab Town" Carlton Mellick III — Radiation fetishists, balloon people, mutant crabs, sail-bike road warriors, and a love affair between a woman and an H-Bomb. This is one mean asshole of a city. Welcome to Crab Town. **100 pages $8**

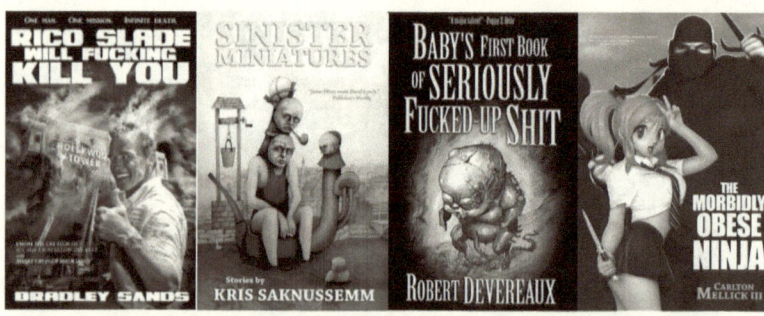

BB-119 "Rico Slade Will Fucking Kill You" Bradley Sands — Rico Slade is an action hero. Rico Slade can rip out a throat with his bare hands. Rico Slade's favorite food is the honey-roasted peanut. Rico Slade will fucking kill everyone. A novel. **122 pages $8**

BB-120 "Sinister Miniatures" Kris Saknussemm — The definitive collection of short fiction by Kris Saknussemm, confirming that he is one of the best, most daring writers of the weird to emerge in the twenty-first century. **180 pages $11**

BB-121 "Baby's First Book of Seriously Fucked up Shit" Robert Devereaux — Ten stories of the strange, the gross, and the just plain fucked up from one of the most original voices in horror. **176 pages $11**

BB-122 "The Morbidly Obese Ninja" Carlton Mellick III — These days, if you want to run a successful company . . . you're going to need a lot of ninjas. **92 pages $8**

BB-123 **"Abortion Arcade" Cameron Pierce** — An intoxicating blend of body horror and midnight movie madness, reminiscent of early David Lynch and the splatterpunks at their most sublime. **172 pages $11**

BB-124 **"Black Hole Blues" Patrick Wensink** — A hilarious double helix of country music and physics. **196 pages $11**

BB-125 **"Barbarian Beast Bitches of the Badlands" Carlton Mellick III** — Three prequels and sequels to *Warrior Wolf Women of the Wasteland*. **284 pages $13**

BB-126 **"The Traveling Dildo Salesman" Kevin L. Donihe** — A nightmare comedy about destiny, faith, and sex toys. Also featuring Donihe's most lurid and infamous short stories: *Milky Agitation, Two-Way Santa, The Helen Mower, Living Room Zombies,* and *Revenge of the Living Masturbation Rag*. **108 pages $8**

BB-127 **"Metamorphosis Blues" Bruce Taylor** — Enter a land of love beasts, intergalactic cowboys, and rock 'n roll. A land where Sears Catalogs are doorways to insanity and men keep mysterious black boxes. Welcome to the monstrous mind of Mr. Magic Realism. **136 pages $11**

BB-128 **"The Driver's Guide to Hitting Pedestrians" Andersen Prunty** — A pocket guide to the twenty-three most painful things in life, written by the most well-adjusted man in the universe. **108 pages $8**

BB-129 **"Island of the Super People" Kevin Shamel** — Four students and their anthropology professor journey to a remote island to study its indigenous population. But this is no ordinary native culture. They're super heroes and villains with flesh costumes and out-landish abilities like self-detonation, musical eyelashes, and microwave hands. **194 pages $11**

BB-130 **"Fantastic Orgy" Carlton Mellick III** — Shark Sex, mutant cats, and strange sexually transmitted diseases. Featuring the stories: *Candy-coated, Ear Cat, Fantastic Orgy, City Hobgoblins,* and *Porno in August*. **136 pages $9**

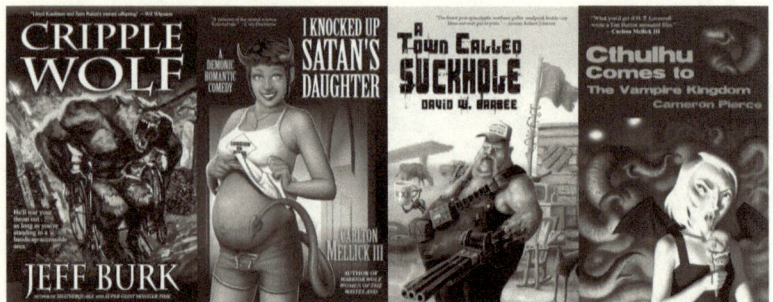

BB-131 **"Cripple Wolf" Jeff Burk** — Part man. Part wolf. 100% crippled. Also including *Punk Rock Nursing Home, Adrift with Space Badgers, Cook for Your Life, Just Another Day in the Park, Frosty and the Full Monty,* and *House of Cats.* **152 pages $10**

BB-132 **"I Knocked Up Satan's Daughter" Carlton Mellick III** — An adorable, violent, fantastical love story. A romantic comedy for the bizarro fiction reader. **152 pages $10**

BB-133 **"A Town Called Suckhole" David W. Barbee** — Far into the future, in the nuclear bowels of post-apocalyptic Dixie, there is a town. A town of derelict mobile homes, ancient junk, and mutant wildlife. A town of slack jawed rednecks who bask in the splendors of moonshine and mud boggin'. A town dedicated to the bloody and demented legacy of the Old South. A town called Suckhole. **144 pages $10**

BB-134 **"Cthulhu Comes to the Vampire Kingdom" Cameron Pierce** — What you'd get if H. P. Lovecraft wrote a Tim Burton animated film. **148 pages $11**

BB-135 **"I am Genghis Cum" Violet LeVoit** — From the savage Arctic tundra to post-partum mutations to your missing daughter's unmarked grave, join visionary madwoman Violet LeVoit in this non-stop eight-story onslaught of full-tilt Bizarro punk lit thrills. **124 pages $9**

BB-136 **"Haunt" Laura Lee Bahr** — A tripping-balls Los Angeles noir, where a mysterious dame drags you through a time-warping Bizarro hall of mirrors. **316 pages $13**

BB-137 **"Amazing Stories of the Flying Spaghetti Monster" edited by Cameron Pierce** — Like an all-spaghetti evening of Adult Swim, the Flying Spaghetti Monster will show you the many realms of His Noodly Appendage. Learn of those who worship him and the lives he touches in distant, mysterious ways. **228 pages $12**

BB-138 **"Wave of Mutilation" Douglas Lain** — A dream-pop exploration of modern architecture and the American identity, *Wave of Mutilation* is a Zen finger trap for the 21st century. **100 pages $8**

BB-139 **"Hooray for Death!" Mykle Hansen** — Famous Author Mykle Hansen draws unconventional humor from deaths tiny and large, and invites you to laugh while you can. **128 pages $10**

BB-140 **"Hypno-hog's Moonshine Monster Jamboree" Andrew Goldfarb** — Hicks, Hogs, Horror! Goldfarb is back with another strange illustrated tale of backwoods weirdness. **120 pages $9**

BB-141 **"Broken Piano For President" Patrick Wensink** — A comic masterpiece about the fast food industry, booze, and the necessity to choose happiness over work and security. **372 pages $15**

BB-142 **"Please Do Not Shoot Me in the Face" Bradley Sands** — A novel in three parts, *Please Do Not Shoot Me in the Face: A Novel*, is the story of one boy detective, the worst ninja in the world, and the great American fast food wars. It is a novel of loss, destruction, and--incredibly--genuine hope. **224 pages $12**

BB-143 **"Santa Steps Out" Robert Devereaux** — Sex, Death, and Santa Claus ... The ultimate erotic Christmas story is back. **294 pages $13**

BB-144 **"Santa Conquers the Homophobes" Robert Devereaux** — "I wish I could hope to ever attain one-thousandth the perversity of Robert Devereaux's toenail clippings." - Poppy Z. Brite **316 pages $13**

BB-145 **"We Live Inside You" Jeremy Robert Johnson** — "Jeremy Robert Johnson is dancing to a way different drummer. He loves language, he loves the edge, and he loves us people. These stories have range and style and wit. This is entertainment... and literature."- Jack Ketchum **188 pages $11**

BB-146 **"Clockwork Girl" Athena Villaverde** — Urban fairy tales for the weird girl in all of us. Like a combination of Francesca Lia Block, Charles de Lint, Kathe Koja, Tim Burton, and Hayao Miyazaki, her stories are cute, kinky, edgy, magical, provocative, and strange, full of poetic imagery and vicious sexuality. **160 pages $10**

BB-147 **"Armadillo Fists" Carlton Mellick III** — A weird-as-hell gangster story set in a world where people drive giant mechanical dinosaurs instead of cars. **168 pages $11**

BB-148 **"Gargoyle Girls of Spider Island" Cameron Pierce** — Four college seniors venture out into open waters for the tropical party weekend of a lifetime. Instead of a teenage sex fantasy, they find themselves in a nightmare of pirates, sharks, and sex-crazed monsters. **100 pages $8**

BB-149 **"The Handsome Squirm" by Carlton Mellick III** — Like Franz Kafka's *The Trial* meets an erotic body horror version of *The Blob*. **158 pages $11**

BB-150 **"Tentacle Death Trip" Jordan Krall** — It's *Death Race 2000* meets H. P. Lovecraft in bizarro author Jordan Krall's best and most suspenseful work to date. **224 pages $12**

BB-151 **"The Obese" Nick Antosca** — Like Alfred Hitchcock's *The Birds*... but with obese people. **108 pages $10**

BB-152 **"All-Monster Action!" Cody Goodfellow** — The world gave him a blank check and a demand: Create giant monsters to fight our wars. But Dr. Otaku was not satisfied with mere chaos and mass destruction.... **216 pages $12**

BB-153 **"Ugly Heaven" Carlton Mellick III** — Heaven is no longer a paradise. It was once a blissful utopia full of wonders far beyond human comprehension. But the afterlife is now in ruins. It has become an ugly, lonely wasteland populated by strange monstrous beasts, masturbating angels, and sad man-like beings wallowing in the remains of the once-great Kingdom of God. **106 pages $8**

BB-154 **"Space Walrus" Kevin L. Donihe** — Walter is supposed to go where no walrus has ever gone before, but all this astronaut walrus really wants is to take it easy on the intense training, escape the chimpanzee bullies, and win the love of his human trainer Dr. Stephanie. **160 pages $11**

BB-155 **"Unicorn Battle Squad" Kirsten Alene** — Mutant unicorns. A palace with a thousand human legs. The most powerful army on the planet. **192 pages $11**

BB-156 **"Kill Ball" Carlton Mellick III** — In a city where all humans live inside of plastic bubbles, exotic dancers are being murdered in the rubbery streets by a mysterious stalker known only as Kill Ball. **134 pages $10**

BB-157 **"Die You Doughnut Bastards" Cameron Pierce** — The bacon storm is rolling in. We hear the grease and sugar beat against the roof and windows. The doughnut people are attacking. We press close together, forgetting for a moment that we hate each other. **196 pages $11**

BB-158 **"Tumor Fruit" Carlton Mellick III** — Eight desperate castaways find themselves stranded on a mysterious deserted island. They are surrounded by poisonous blue plants and an ocean made of acid. Ravenous creatures lurk in the toxic jungle. The ghostly sound of crying babies can be heard on the wind. **310 pages $13**

BB-159 **"Thunderpussy" David W. Barbee** — When it comes to high-tech global espionage, only one man has the balls to save humanity from the world's most powerful bastards. He's Declan Magpie Bruce, Agent 00X. **136 pages $11**

BB-160 **"Papier Mâché Jesus" Kevin L. Donihe** — Donihe's surreal wit and beautiful mind-bending imagination is on full display with stories such as All Children Go to Hell, Happiness is a Warm Gun, and Swimming in Endless Night. **154 pages $11**

BB-161 **"Cuddly Holocaust" Carlton Mellick III** — The war between humans and toys has come to an end. The toys won. **172 pages $11**

BB-162 **"Hammer Wives" Carlton Mellick III** — Fish-eyed mutants, oceans of insects, and flesh-eating women with hammers for heads. Hammer Wives collects six of his most popular novelettes and short stories. **152 pages $10**